The Lake District Collection

REBECCA HOLMES

Cover photograph : Coniston Water

These stories are works of fiction

Published by Golden Gage Publishing

First published 2016

Author : Rebecca Holmes

With many thanks to Shirley E Blair for her invaluable guidance and advice.

To my family

Twelve stories of love, family and friendship by Rebecca Holmes, a regular writer of fiction for national magazines.

All these stories have previously been published in the People's Friend magazine. If you enjoy warm-hearted stories with a satisfying ending, then this collection is for you.

'Rebecca Holmes is a favourite writer with People's Friend readers, always promising an entertaining, satisfying story with a strong emotional heart and the kind of well-developed characters that make you care about them.'
Shirley E Blair, Commissioning Fiction Editor, the People's Friend magazine.

CONTENTS

And Little Sister Came Too

"Is it all right if Gemma comes along?"

The question stopped Tom in his tracks. He'd met Steph's eleven-year-old sister several times, and they'd got on well enough. Even now, as he stood on the front doorstep, he could see her peering round the newel post at the bottom of the stairs.

"The thing is," Steph continued as Gemma waved and Tom waved back, "she was supposed to be going round to her friend's house for the day, but they've just phoned. Apparently her friend's come down with something, so the plan's off. Mum and Dad have gone visiting relatives in Yorkshire. I can't leave her on her own."

That was true enough, he supposed. It was just unlucky that it had to happen today of all days.

"No problem." He pushed his disappointment to one side. "Hop aboard."

They'd barely pulled away from the kerb when Gemma's voice piped up from the back.

"Where are we going?"

"Coniston," Tom replied.

"Why not Windermere?"

"It'll be too busy."

"But there's more to do on Windermere."

"I've brought plenty of sandwiches," Steph put in. "We'll have a nice picnic on the shore."

"Any chocolate rolls?"

"Yes, Gemma. Don't worry."

"Why have we got a boat on top of the car?" was the next question.

"It's not a boat, it's a canoe," Tom explained.

"Why have we got a canoe on top of the car?"

"So I can go canoeing on the lake."

"What about Steph?"

7

"I stay on dry land and relax with a book."

"That sounds boring. Never mind, Steph. You'll have me to keep you company, today."

They'd not even got as far as the motorway yet. Tom wondered what state his ears would be in by the time they reached their destination.

He and Steph had been going out for over a year now, and since he'd bought a car they'd enjoyed regular trips to the Lakes. Having gone there for as long as he could remember with his parents and older sisters, he knew the quieter spots, away from the main tourist traps. The last few miles of the route involved tight bends and narrow lanes, but he was used to it. Even the car seemed to know its way by now. Once there, they'd potter about by the lake, Tom on the water and Steph on the shore, and then have a picnic. Afterwards, if there was time and the weather stayed fine, they often walked in the woods rising up the steep slope from the valley.

Today was supposed to have been perfect. He'd got it all planned. A couple of hours messing about on the lake, a picnic, a walk in the woods. And a marriage proposal. After the recent dry spell he could even go down on one knee without getting his jeans soggy. But now all that would have to wait.

Gemma was still talking nineteen to the dozen as they pulled into the small car park among the trees.

"What's a Site of Special Scientific Interest?" she asked, reading a notice as Tom and Stephanie unloaded the canoe.

"What it says," he replied. "Usually it's a habitat for rare species. For instance..."

"What's that mountain over there?"

He sighed. "The Old Man of Coniston. Now, do you think you could...?"

"Not as old as that canoe, I'll bet. Are you sure it'll float? It looks a bit battered."

To give her her due, she did make herself helpful in carting stuff down to the shore, but Tom still heaved a sigh of relief as he skimmed out onto the water. For him, nothing could compare with the sense of peace out on the middle of the lake. Steph found the place soothing, too. He'd often come back to find her lying on the picnic rug, eyes closed, listening to the gentle lapping of the water and the rustling of the trees. He doubted

8

she'd have much chance of doing that today.

Back at base, everything was already set out for their picnic lunch. Evidently food was the best thing for keeping chatterboxes quiet and Steph, presumably wise to this, had brought plenty. The fact that this particular chatterbox was busy with her mobile phone probably helped, too, though Tom noticed she was frowning.

"You might not get anything on that," he told her. "The signal's a bit iffy just here. It's too tucked away."

Interestingly, Gemma seemed relieved at the information. Once the final crumbs had disappeared, she was back to normal, bombarding him with questions. He, in turn, found himself telling her about family trips when he was growing up.

"My dad taught us all how to canoe on this very lake," he explained. "It would probably be frowned on now, but he used to tie a clothes line to the back so he could reel us in if we headed out too far, until we learned to steer properly and roll over in case we capsized. He said it was easier than having to swim out and rescue us."

"Cool! Can you teach me?"

"I suppose so" he answered.

"Great. Let's start now."

"Gemma!" Steph warned. "I said you could only come if you didn't get in the way."

As Gemma's face fell, Steph's comment and the sharpness of her tone suddenly brought back memories of Tom's own childhood, when he'd always seemed to be tagging along behind his sisters. For the first time, he caught a glimpse of the day from Gemma's point of view, and it was as different as seeing the mountains from the middle of the lake instead of from the shore. Rather than going round to her friend's house to do whatever girls of their age did, she'd been offloaded onto a couple who in their turn hadn't reckoned on entertaining her, meaning she had to put up with a grumpier-than-usual older sister and her unknown quantity of a boyfriend. It could hardly be described as anyone's idea of a good time.

"I don't see why not," he said. "You can't go out properly on the water today, because I haven't got a life jacket that fits you properly – or a washing line - but we'll stay in this little bit. If all goes well, next time I'll bring you a jacket and a hard hat."

"What do I want one of those for? It's hardly going to keep my hair dry."

9

"It's to protect you from injury, silly. There are rocks under the water. If you capsized and your head bumped into one of those, it'd turn to mush without a helmet."

"What?" Steph almost dropped the Thermos. "You're not involving my sister in any dangerous activity, are you? Mum and Dad'll have a fit."

"She'll be fine. We won't go beyond waist deep, and I'll be next to her for every second."

Reassured, Steph settled down on the rug with a paperback, while Tom showed Gemma the correct method of getting in and out of the canoe, and how to hold and work the paddle. Then he stayed by her as she went along for a few yards, steadying her when she wobbled, and trying not to laugh as her face was a mask of concentration.

The sun was already sending a golden glow over the mountains when Steph started packing away and looked pointedly at her watch.

"That's enough for today," said Tom, taking the hint. "Don't be surprised if your arms and shoulders ache tomorrow."

"It's been a good day, hasn't it?" Steph commented, back at the car, as they made sure the canoe was safely secured on the roof rack for the homeward journey. "I was worried it would be a wash-out when I found we'd have to take Gemma, but you've been brilliant with her. That canoeing lesson really made her day. She's a lot happier than she was this morning."

Tom wasn't surprised. When he'd been showing her how to use the paddle, Gemma had confided the real reason she hadn't been able to go round to her friend's house. It turned out they'd had an argument about something at school the previous day. The sudden illness had probably been a ruse.

"Well, I think it was," she'd said. "I'm glad in a way. I didn't want to spend all day with Sophie if she was going to be mardy. If I'd said anything to Steph she'd have started asking all sorts of questions, and saying we should tell Mum, and I didn't want to talk about it."

"Sometimes you don't," Tom agreed. "At least, not until you feel ready. I always find problems seem smaller when I'm out here, especially with the mountains all around. They seem to help put everything into perspective. If you feel down, try remembering the things you've done this afternoon. Not many eleven-year-olds get to go canoeing in such

10

amazing scenery."

From the way Gemma's face had brightened, he knew he'd said the right thing. It made him feel better, too, about having to abandon his plans to take his and Steph's relationship a step further.

And yet, now he thought about it, wasn't that what had happened, even if not in quite the way he'd expected? He and Steph had learned they could enjoy a day together, that it could still mean as much to them, in the presence of someone else. They were comfortable enough not to need any special aura of "togetherness" to appreciate each other's company.

Right. That was the final knot checked. Steph had finished all hers, too, getting to be quite an old hand at this by now. Gemma was sitting on a tree stump a few yards away, finally worn out but no doubt plotting more days out and wondering when was the best time to ask.

Which brought him back to his own question.

Perhaps there never was a best time. Perhaps it was often a case of coming right out with it. Wasn't this as good a moment as any, in their favourite place, and with Gemma out of earshot?

"Er, hrrrm." He cleared his throat. "There's something I've been meaning to ask you."

"Hmmm?" Steph shielded her eyes with one hand as she gazed across the road to the glassy surface of the lake visible between the trunks of beeches and silver birch.

"I was wondering if you'd like to - er – marry me?"

As she turned round to look at him, he felt more flustered than ever, but there was no backing out now.

"I was going to ask you during a walk in the woods, go down on one knee and all that. Maybe we could have our reception at that hotel further round the lake? It's the perfect setting." Why was his heart hammering so loudly? "I even thought, if the answer had been 'Yes', that we could call in on the way home and check available dates. That's only if you want to, of course."

Wasn't she going to say anything? Surely she could see he was struggling, here.

"Have I blown it? Should I have waited till another day and done it properly? Or do you not want…?" His voice trailed off.

Tom didn't know how long passed before Stephanie spoke. Probably enough to canoe across the lake and back and have a pint of Bluebird afterwards. That was how it felt, anyway.

11

"Oh, honestly," she said at last. "You daft thing. I don't mind about all the going down on one knee palaver. This feels much more natural. More... *us,* somehow." Her voice sounded different, sort of choked up, and he thought he saw her eyes mist over, but she blinked rapidly a few times and they cleared.

"Gemma," she called, after she'd blown her nose. "Time to get in the car. It'll take us a bit longer to get home. We need to make a detour to sort out a wedding."

"Can I be a bridesmaid?"

"I should imagine so." Tom couldn't stop grinning as they wound down the lane. His face would start aching, at this rate.

"What shall I wear?"

"We'll see," said Steph.

"I don't mind as long as it isn't pink"

She was just suggesting that they could bring the canoe and fill it with flowers, when her mobile phone beeped twice.

"A text message," she squealed.

There was a moment's blissful silence as she read it.

"It's all right," she squealed again. "Sophie's still my friend. She was in a bad mood yesterday because she'd had an argument with her mum. I can't wait to phone her tonight and tell her all the news."

'Me, too,' thought Tom as they pulled up outside an old manor house overlooking the lake. He was pretty sure their families would be even more excited than Gemma. As for the canoe, after the part it had played today, maybe it should come to the wedding. He wasn't so sure about the flowers, but they'd cross that bridge when they came to it.

Walking Boots and Poetry Books

"This cottage is perfect." Julia glanced round at the rooms that were to be their home from home over the next few days, taking in the log burner, and the "welcome" wine and flowers on the small pine dining table. "Just look at that view. We won't even have to get out of bed in the mornings to see the lake, or those trees on the far bank. They're such a vivid shade of green. I'm glad we opted for a spring wedding."

"Same here," Stuart agreed. He hesitated. "Are you sure you don't mind that we couldn't afford somewhere more exotic for our honeymoon? Perhaps if we'd waited another year, we might have been able to stretch to the extra expense."

"Probably not that much extra," Julia pointed out. "Anyway, we both love the Lake District, so in a lot of ways it makes sense that the first time we visit it together should be the start of our married life." She unzipped her suitcase. "Come on, the sooner we get this lot unpacked, the sooner we can walk down to the village and explore. I spotted a very nice-looking café near the church on the way here."

The next few minutes passed in relative silence as they got on with the job in hand. Julia had brought a selection of warm clothes to cope with a week of typical Lakeland weather, along with waterproofs and gloves. Stuart's being a veteran of holidays in the area was also borne out by the items he unpacked. For all that, she couldn't help doing a double-take when he lifted a carrier bag out of his suitcase.

"I thought I'd better use a plastic bag to stop the boots getting everything else filthy," he explained, as he saw her watching.

"Are those walking boots?" she asked.

"Of course they are. What did you expect? Ballet shoes?"

"No, but I haven't seen those before. I mean, I've seen walking boots, obviously, just not yours. They look very… serious."

"How else did you think I'd go fell-walking? They're a bit battered, but they're a good brand, so they've got plenty of life left in them yet. Haven't you brought yours?"

13

Julia held up her walking shoes – or what had always served the purpose up till now. They were good, strong shoes, fine for general use, but …

Stuart shook his head. "Those might just about be okay for well-made paths on the lower slopes and by some of the lake shores, but I don't know how you've coped with them on the fells."

When Julia replied, she was aware her voice sounded small.

"My family didn't go fell-walking."

"What? How can you come here and not walk on the fells?"

"There are plenty of other things to do, like seeing the different lakes and tarns, for instance. I've had some lovely walks round some of them. Then there are the houses where famous poets and writers lived. The week isn't complete without visiting at least one of those." As if to support her argument, she lifted several novels and volumes of poetry out of her suitcase.

"No wonder you were huffing and puffing, dragging that lot up the stairs," said Stuart, when he saw them. "You should have got me to carry it."

"I managed, didn't I? Just because we're married, that doesn't make me suddenly weak and helpless. I always bring something to read in the Lakes. It goes with the place."

"As do walking boots." Stuart sighed. "It looks like we've both been so busy preparing for the wedding, as well as our everyday lives, that we didn't take time to sit down and discuss our plans for this week."

"I suppose most people just plan to relax and sunbathe, and maybe fit in a bit of sight-seeing, on their honeymoons," Jess said. "At least, I imagine they do. I've never really asked them."

"Me neither. Funnily enough, you don't do a lot of sunbathing in the Lake District, unless you're very lucky. Still, I suppose that leaves the other two."

Who would have thought their ideas of a Lakeland holiday would have differed so much? Julia wondered. She remembered her own previous trips here with her parents and two sisters. They'd had so many happy times, staying in a variety of cottages, usually on the edge of one or other of the villages nestling under different fells, each with their own special character and atmosphere.

Obviously, a lot people visited the area with the main purpose of

14

going on the mountains. She'd often seen groups heading up the beginnings of steep tracks, with bulging rucksacks on their backs and determined expressions on their faces. Whether the prospect of tackling such expeditions with three little girls in tow had been too daunting for her parents, she didn't know. It was certainly true that, while being reasonably fit, their idea of gentle exercise hadn't extended to tackling precipitous paths and slippery scree slopes. The cost of kitting out all five of them with the correct equipment on a family budget would hardly have been an encouragement, either, and they wouldn't have risked fell walking without it. Everyone knew too many accidents happened that way.

Instead, there'd been countless picnics by lakes, boat rides and visits to places such as Beatrix Potter's - and therefore Peter Rabbit's – home, progressing to those of more "grown up" famous Cumbrian sons and daughters, until Julia and her sisters began to feel almost like honorary Lakeland daughters, themselves.

She'd been round Dove Cottage and Rydal Mount so many times, not only did she reckon she could find her way with her eyes closed, but almost felt as if she knew the Wordsworths personally. Afternoons spent at Brantwood unfailingly left her with a sense of peace, combined with awe, whether at the breath-taking views over Coniston Water and the Old Man, its best-known mountain, or the achievements of the house's famous owner, John Ruskin.

She'd assumed Stuart's experiences had been similar, and it seemed he'd thought the same about her. Now she realised they'd never really got round to going into a lot of detail about their respective family holidays. Having said that, they'd both known the names of many of the mountains and argued the comparative qualities of Eskdale, Langdale and Borrowdale, so perhaps their assumptions weren't so surprising, after all.

Yet, for two people about to embark on the rest of their lives together, shouldn't they have shared more?

That seemed to be Stuart's sentiment, too, as they waited for their food in the café Julia had noticed earlier. The place lived up to its expectations, being warm, clean and friendly, with a fire blazing away in a slate hearth.

"It's just that you'd think we'd be better at communicating with each other. Then we'd have realised we both like doing different things and planned accordingly." He smiled ruefully. "It doesn't bode very well, does it, for the start of our married life?"

Julia thought about it for a moment. "I suppose most married couples hardly know each other at first. Unless they've been going out for years and years before they tie the knot, the time before their wedding is only a small fraction of their overall life together. My parents had only known each other for a year before they got married, and they've just celebrated their twenty-fifth wedding anniversary. Given the lives we live on a day-to-day basis, it's hardly surprising that all this didn't really come up." She giggled. "Let's face it, you'd get more than a few odd looks if you wore your walking boots in the city centre, wouldn't you? It isn't as though you had a load of mountaineering magazines lying around, either. We're individuals, so we're bound be different, in all sorts of ways. It's how we cope with the differences that matters."

Stuart seemed to cheer up, though whether that was due to what she'd just said, or thanks to their plates of Cumberland sausages and chips arriving, Julia wasn't entirely sure.

"You're right," he said, sprinkling vinegar on his chips. "Now I think about it, not many people expect to spend their honeymoon striding over mountains. If you're not up to it, you can end up aching in places you never knew you had, which wouldn't be fair on you. We'll go for the gentler options, this holiday. It's time I saw the Lakes from a new perspective, anyway."

They soon settled into a routine, which wasn't difficult in the refurbished former copper miner's cottage. Long, lazy breakfasts were enjoyed in the living room, overlooking the lake. With the evenings still being chilly, and a generous supply of logs in the wicker basket by the fireplace, Julia and Stuart made full use of the opportunity to get cosy. She'd put her feet up with one of her books, while he pored over Ordnance Survey maps.

Trips to Julia's favourite houses were undertaken, and she enjoyed introducing him to places she'd come to regard as old friends. If he was restless for the fells, he hid it well. The fact that rain and mist blanketed them on most days doubtless played its part. Thankfully, that didn't dampen their spirits.

"If there's one thing I've learned over the years, it's that you've got to accept the climate as part of the place," Stuart remarked.

The weather wasn't all gloomy. They managed boat trips on Windermere, and woodland walks, by gentle, bluebell-swathed slopes.

"It's as if an artist chose blue paint instead of the usual green," Julia commented. "I've always found that surreal."

What also felt surreal was the way the outside world and all its concerns could almost not have existed. It gave them the chance to really talk and simply be together, in a way that had never been quite possible before.

At Keswick, they strolled by Derwent Water, followed by a meander round the shops, adding to the host of memories they'd crammed into a few days. Even better, as the morning progressed, the skies cleared and the sun came out, setting the nearby fells glowing in the new light. Skiddaw, especially, was so sharply defined, it looked as if it had quietly moved closer to the town it sheltered, using the cover of the earlier mists.

"The views from up there would be perfect on a day like this. Layer after layer of mountains, and the water reflecting it all like a mirror." The words seemed to escape from Stuart's mouth almost before he realised it, as the couple lunched on home-made soup at a little café in one of the tiny alleyways leading off the market square.

Julia couldn't help an amused smile. "Does a bit of sunshine always make you wax lyrical, up here?" she asked.

"Sorry." Stuart smiled back. "Force of habit, thinking about being up on the fells. It's true, though. The views would be amazing." He hesitated before continuing. "If we come here again, which I'm sure we will, do you think you might perhaps give fell-walking a go? I've enjoyed doing different things this week, but you might appreciate trying something different, too. I wouldn't expect you to go charging up Scafell Pike, or anything like that, but there are plenty of less demanding routes, and you're reasonably fit, so they wouldn't cause you any problems."

"Only reasonably fit? Thanks for the vote of confidence." Julia tried her best to look offended.

Stuart grinned. "You're welcome."

"See? We must know each other pretty well, to take that as a joke. Or was it a joke?" she added, teasingly. "I may have been genuinely put out by your remark."

"As if. Seriously, though, if we were here again, would you consider it?"

"Oh, I think I can do better than that," she replied. "You've been so sweet to me this week, going round all those places without a single complaint. Well, apart from stifling the odd yawn."

17

"To be fair, it wasn't really walking weather," he pointed out. "And it's made me see another side of the Lakes that I'd never really got into before." He frowned as Julia leaned down and took her phone out of her bag. "What is it? Have you got a text message?"

"No, I'm checking the weather forecast. It's handy, this café having a wi-fi connection. Ah, here we are, and it's just as I thought. We're finally in for some good weather over the next couple of days." She showed him the screen. "You've let me show you the things that I like, but I know you're dying to get up into those hills, so I think it's time I returned the favour. Nothing too difficult, mind. Just enough to see some of those views you keep getting all poetic about."

Stuart positively beamed. "You'd do that for me?"

"Of course I would, silly. Anyway, going round some of these places has reminded me that Wordsworth and Coleridge used to walk miles over the fells. What was good enough for them is good enough for me."

"Right." Her husband pushed his now-empty soup bowl to one side. "It's too late to set out anywhere now, but when we get back to the cottage, I'll look at the maps and plan a route. Bearing in mind what you've just said, I've already got a pretty good idea of where we might go. Before that, though, we need to get you the proper footwear, so you don't end up with a broken ankle, or worse. It's just as well there are plenty of outdoor-wear shops here."

"Do you mean you're going shoe shopping with me?" Julia raised her eyebrows.

"No, not shoe shopping. Walking boot shopping."

As they paused to take in the view over Grasmere and Rydal Water, the next day, Julia truly began to appreciate why Stuart was so passionate about fell-walking. She appreciated, too, his insistence, the previous evening, that she walk around the cottage in her new walking boots, to get used to them. She never usually wore anything this heavy, yet there was no doubt they were perfect for the job. Even though this route, in the heart of Wordsworth territory, was a relatively easy one, there had been a couple of points where she'd probably have gone over on her ankle without the support of these near-magical boots. She was sure the lower part of her feet would have been aching by now, too, without the miracle of shock-absorbing soles.

"Something tells me I'll be glad of a hot bath tonight," she said.

"And we've still got about another hour and a half to go," Stuart told her. "Just think how wonderfully toned your legs are going to be."

It was a day of discoveries. Julia had thought she knew this particular region of the Lake District inside out. And so she did, but only at ground level.

"Everything looks so different from up here," she commented, as they topped another rise. "We've hardly even met another soul."

"I knew you'd like it, as soon as I read in one of the guides that it was a favourite with William and Dorothy Wordsworth." He stopped and held out his arms, as if declaiming to an invisible audience. "*I wandered lonely as a cloud.* There you are, you've even got me quoting poetry."

"Now you're being silly." Julia pushed him playfully. "For one thing, you're not alone, you're with me. For another, clouds don't tend to be lonely, round here. That wasn't one of William's better poems, anyway, bless him."

"It's sort of appropriate today, though. Look at that blue sky. Who could ask for more? I know we're not on the summit of a mountain, but at times like this I feel like I'm on top of the world, as well as being with the person I most want to share it with. We might both enjoy different things, but we can still make the effort and enjoy them together." His expression became more serious as he took her hand and drew her close to him. "Here's hoping for more weeks like this. Lots and lots."

It was just as well there was no-one else around, apart from a few sheep, as their kiss lingered and Julia felt herself melt in his arms. Afterwards, they stood for a few moments, their arms wrapped round each other, her head on his shoulder. Yet again, she had the sense that their everyday life had been left far, far behind.

But it would be their everyday life that would count in the years ahead, buoyed up by precious memories laid down at times like this. It wouldn't just be love that got them through, she realised, but other things, as well. Like the skill they'd learned this week, on how to compromise.

When they drew apart, Stuart looked at his watch. "We'd better get moving before the light starts to fade. I don't know about you, but I'll be ready for a hot drink when we've finished."

"It's funny you should say that," Julia replied. "I happen to know a place that serves a perfect hot chocolate, complete with marshmallows."

A Perfect Day For A Stroll

"You, Heather, are the original hopeless romantic."

My sister's words ran through my mind as I checked my appearance in a handbag mirror on the final stage of my journey. I'm not normally vain, but today I wanted to look my best. Luckily the other passengers in the compartment had disembarked at a previous station, so I had it to myself as the train puffed towards Westmorland and the scenery became more hilly with each passing mile.

I was used to hills, of course, coming as I did from a Lancashire mill town surrounded by moorland. Still, however much I loved the moors, they couldn't compare to proper mountains, especially on a day like this, with a clear blue sky. At least my sister wouldn't be able to joke about me having my head in the clouds.

We'd both found it even more of a joke that it should be Rosamund, two years younger than me and definitely not a hopeless romantic, who'd married first. Steady, likeable Charles had almost certainly been drawn to her down-to-earth, common sense approach to life, as well as her other assets.

I was looking forward to seeing her. The last time had been almost three months ago, at her wedding, which had been a truly memorable event despite the restrictions of rationing, still in force even though the war was over. Yet, if I was honest with myself, an equally large part of me was looking forward to seeing Edward. Hence the extra attention to my appearance.

Ever since Rosamund had invited me, I'd been planning what to wear on this trip. Several late nights had gone into re-styling an old floral blouse to go with my favourite skirt, and I was wearing my nicest shoes, of the same dark blue as my skirt, with an eyelet pattern all round the border, and heels high enough for elegance yet not quite too high for comfort.

All in all, it promised to be a perfect day for a stroll by the lake, with arguably the finest views in England thrown in for good measure.

The whistle of the train as it pulled into Windermere station jolted me from my thoughts. As I prepared to leave, I could already glimpse the smiling faces of Rosamund and Charles looking out for me. And, with them, Edward.

When I stepped down onto the platform, however, my heart stilled its agreeable fluttering and my own smile died on my lips. All of them were wearing warm pullovers and trousers, and sturdy-looking boots. Even Rosamund's long, wavy hair was pinned back in a bun. Judging by the healthy glow to her complexion, married life suited her. No doubt the fresh air and breathtaking countryside around Bowness, where Charles was a junior solicitor in his father's firm, also helped.

They both frowned in unison as I approached.

"There must be some mistake," Rosamund, never one to avoid the subject, said once we'd hugged. "I'm sure I mentioned a walk when I wrote."

"You did," I replied, "but I thought you just meant walking down by the lake and taking in the scenery."

I paused while Charles gave me a warm, brotherly peck on the cheek. When Edward then stepped forward and shook my hand, my heart started fluttering again and I could feel my complexion colouring until it must surely compete with my sister's.

Edward had been Charles's best man at the wedding. Within minutes of our being introduced, I'd felt as if I'd known him for much longer. The number of dances for which he'd partnered me, made me wonder if he felt the same, and I'd been unable to stop thinking about his gentle brown eyes and quiet smile ever since.

What must he think of me now, turning up so ill equipped? It hardly made a good impression.

That seemed to be Rosamund's reaction.

"Trust you to get the wrong end of the stick. Charles saved his petrol rations specially so we could all have a day in the mountains."

"Now, my love," Charles said. "Heather is our guest. There will be other days for walking on the fells."

But not as glorious as this. Even though my sister didn't say them out loud, I could almost hear the words hanging in the air.

I couldn't blame Rosamund for being annoyed. It was my fault for getting carried away in the excitement of anticipating the trip, when I should have been well aware of what her interpretation of "a walk" round here was likely to entail.

Yet were my clothes really a problem? Not if I could help it!

"We can still go," I said. "I've coped often enough on the moors when I wasn't correctly dressed, and they aren't exactly a gentle stroll."

"True enough," my sister conceded. "So long as you're sure. Just don't blame me if it goes wrong."

Of course it wouldn't. I'd lost count of the number of times I'd set off on a whim, wearing a dress, and ended up walking for miles, even scrambling up rocky outcrops so that I could see the coast in the distance on a clear day.

I'd lost count, too, of the number of times my mother had shaken her head in despair at such impetuous behaviour.

Soon we were all in Charles's car, driving up and up a steep, winding road between dry stone walls, then down again, into a valley with mountains towering over us on either side, before coming to stop down a narrow lane.

"Here we are," said Rosamund. "Helvellyn."

How I loved that name, with its hint of untold legends and a poetry all of its own. Poetry or not, that didn't change the fact that we were looking up at one of the largest among the Lakeland mountains. No wonder the others were all wearing their sturdiest boots.

The first part was tolerable enough, probably because it followed an old pony track, according to Charles. Walking at a comfortable pace, Rosamund and I were able to catch up on each other's news. One of the nice things about being sisters was that, however much we may argue, we were always there for each other.

That wasn't enough to take my mind off the fact that Edward was walking on ahead with Charles and had hardly seemed to notice me since greeting me at the station. This day wasn't turning out as I'd hoped.

After a while, we came to a more demanding section, where we all had to concentrate more closely. I blessed my experience of tackling the wilder parts of the moors from an early age. It meant coping with awkward terrain was second nature.

They say pride goes before a fall, and it did here. Or almost. I stumbled on some awkwardly angled rocks and briefly lost my balance. Although I grabbed on to a tussock of grass, that didn't stop one of my shoes falling right off my foot.

23

Both Rosamund and I lunged to rescue it, but in vain. All we could do was watch as it bounced and skittered down, before coming to rest on the slope several yards below, its descent halted only thanks to a gorse bush that, like the hardiest of sheep, somehow thrived in this inhospitable place while its cousins had the sense to settle on lower ground.

Rosamund's nagging, supposedly sensible half came to the fore again. She sighed heavily.

"I might have known this would happen. Wait here."

It goes without saying that I wasn't prepared to suffer the indignity of watching my little sister rescue my shoe. I clambered down with her, trying not to wince as stones poked into my stockinged foot.

Somehow we both got there safely, even though at times we ended up clinging to the slope like a pair of monkeys, or sliding inelegantly down scree where it slipped beneath us.

It took a fair bit of cautious manoeuvring to avoid the prickles and retrieve the shoe, but we managed it. I popped it back onto my by now worse-for-wear foot, and was just about to follow Rosamund, when something stopped me. That dratted gorse bush had caught my skirt.

By now I'd completely lost my patience. Instead of doing the sensible thing and extricating myself slowly and carefully, I gave a hard tug, to be rewarded by the sound of ripping cloth.

I am sorry to say that over the next few seconds a torrent of extremely unladylike language escaped me. When I'd finished, Rosamund and I stood staring at each other in stunned silence before we both burst out laughing.

Only when we stopped did we notice two heads peering over the ridge above us.

"I say, are you two all right?" Charles called.

"Of course we are. Don't worry," Rosamund answered. "One of Heather's shoes came off, that's all."

That wasn't quite true. Still, I managed find a safety pin in my bag, which we used to hold my skirt and what remained of my dignity together.

As we caught up with the men, I realised that Edward hadn't said a thing throughout the recent exchange. What if he'd heard my outburst and been shocked by it? Could the day get any worse?

Our climb continued uneventfully until, after a while, our party stopped at the foot of what could only be described as a tower of rock looming up before us.

Rosamund stood with her hands on her hips and chin jutting out. "The approach to Striding Edge," she said. "I've been looking forward to this all year."

Striding Edge? I'd heard of that before. It was famous. Or, rather, infamous, being a narrow ridge of jagged rock across the crest of the mountain. "Scrambling Over And Hanging On For Dear Life Edge" might be a more appropriate name.

Normally I would have relished the challenge. With today's perfect conditions, the ridge should pose no real problems to an experienced walker in the correct footwear.

That was the point. I may have been impetuous, but there was a huge gap between that and being reckless. I could have kicked myself.

Although other mountains and fells stretched out in a dramatic panorama all around us, I was in too much of a dilemma to appreciate them. It seemed the only sensible thing was for me to make my way slowly and humiliatingly back while rest carried on.

"I have to admit I'm somewhat wary of going along the top."

I looked round, surprised, at the sound of Edward's voice.

"Bit of a dickey leg, I'm afraid," he added. "Courtesy of the war. There's an easier path a little lower. If anyone would like to keep me company on that, they'd be more than welcome."

He smiled in my direction. I couldn't remember his leg troubling him when we'd danced together at the wedding, but I knew many young men had continuing problems from wartime injuries, so I silently ticked myself off for being uncharitable.

"I'll go with you," I said. "I think Striding Edge might be a little ambitious for me today."

Thankfully, everyone found that amusing. Rosamund looked visibly relieved, which I supposed was understandable. She could hardly have relished the prospect of telling our parents that their older daughter had managed to fall off a mountain.

We went our separate ways. At first, Edward and I walked in silence.

"I can hardly believe how time has flown since your sister's wedding," Edward said after a few minutes. "I suppose you must miss her?"

"I do in some ways," I admitted. "But during the last couple of years we've both lived our own lives, especially once she was working away from home. I hope you enjoyed the wedding?" I ventured.

"I had an excellent time. Mainly thanks to you, I might add. Normally I'm terrible at those sorts of events. I'm not much of a conversationalist, you see."

I laughed. "I'm the same. I'd much rather be walking on the moors than standing around in a dance hall."

"Yes, I caught a glimpse of them from the churchyard after we came out of the service." He helped me over a slightly tricky section. I was quite happy to let him, and not only because it was probably best to play safe today. "They seemed to have their own bleak beauty."

"They do. I'm even named after them. When I was born, my parents called me after the heather that grows there."

I was soon telling him all about my favourite walks.

"No wonder you've coped so well," Edward said. "You've clearly had plenty of practice."

"You wouldn't have thought it, from my performance today."

"Oh, I don't know. You got this far without too many mishaps, didn't you? And provided some entertainment in the process." His lips twitched.

"Oh dear. You mean you heard me?"

"I suspect you could have been heard half way across the county. Don't worry. Any red-blooded walker would have reacted in exactly the same way. We're not easily offended up here."

"Somehow I don't think I'll ever be wearing these shoes again." I looked down at them ruefully. My poor, beautiful shoes were almost unrecognisable. Their rich blue was now a muddy grey, and I wasn't sure how it had happened, but one of the heels had come askew. Then there was the state of my skirt. "I'm not exactly elegant."

"I think you'd look wonderful whatever you were wearing," Edward said gallantly as I pulled a face. He cleared his throat. "And I thought exactly the same when I met you at your sister's wedding."

We rejoined Rosamund and Charles when the paths converged.

Rosamund beamed at us.

"That was marvellous. You really must bring some decent walking boots with you next time, Heather. You should try it too, Edward, when your leg's better," she added, looking rather intently at him, I thought.

Eventually we returned to the car and drove back to Windermere, where we all agreed we deserved a treat, and made a beeline for the nearest tea room.

"The owner here performs miracles with what's available," Rosamund said as we arrived. "The cakes have to be seen to be believed."

Soon Edward and I were laughing together at all sorts of little, seemingly inconsequential things.

"There's one thing I don't understand," I said, when I was sure the others weren't listening. "If you felt the same about me as I did about you at the wedding, couldn't you have written to me? My sister would have given you my address."

"I wasn't sure whether you really felt that way, or whether you were just enjoying the celebrations. And, to be fair, is letter reading really your strong point?" He raised his eyebrows, and I felt myself blushing. "You may or may not be aware of this," he continued, "but it was Rosamund's idea that we all have a day out. And I think I'd better not say any more, because she might hear me."

I'd be quizzing my sister on the point later. But at that moment, with a waitress placing a fully laden cake stand on the table between us, I was more interested in both the sweetness of its contents and of life itself.

A hopeless romantic? Maybe, but it seemed the day had turned out to be perfect, after all.

The Call of the Mountains

Spring was Rachel's favourite time of year in the Lake District, the season when everything came back to life after winter. New grass, emerald in the strengthening sun, slowly spread its way up the brown slopes of the mountains, some still snow-capped. Daffodils brightened roadside verges, and in patches of woodland a violet haze announced the bluebells were in flower.

It was also the time when bookings picked up at the Bed and Breakfast she ran on the farm.

"It's wonderful here," guests commented as they looked out of the window. "The view of those mountains is breathtaking."

"They're the Langdale Pikes," she'd tell those who didn't already know. "I always looked out for them on day trips here as a child. They never failed to cheer me up, whatever the weather."

Even now, when she saw their craggy brows almost constantly from the farm, they still made her smile, and with good reason. Matt had proposed on the summit there, two years ago. He'd had it all planned, he told her later. Unfortunately, he hadn't planned it quite carefully enough to take account of the wet spring. The right knee of his jeans had got soaked through when he'd inadvertently knelt in a boggy patch to pop the question.

"Well, I didn't want to kneel on a rocky bit," he said afterwards. "That would have been too painful if you'd kept me waiting for an answer."

Rachel never tired of telling the story to guests as she served them breakfast at the oak table in the dining room.

"I was really nervous you'd say no," Matt had admitted, at the time. "Farm life out here is going to be a massive change for you. I even wondered whether it was fair to ask you."

Although Rachel had grown up in a sleepy little town not far away, student life at eighteen, followed by a job, had drawn her to the bright lights of the city. Coming back more or less to where she'd come from would seem a backward step to many, and becoming a farmer's wife even more so.

"That's the back of beyond!" her flat mate and best friend, Kate, had exclaimed. "Aren't you worried you'll miss everything you're giving up here?"

If she hadn't met Matt at a young farmer's disco she'd been invited to when visiting home one weekend, the question may well have never arisen, but Rachel had no regrets. Sometimes she'd lay a hand, palm flat, against one of the walls, to feel the cool stone against her warm skin. It was a trick Rosemary, Matt's mother, had told her about.

"I know it sounds strange, but it helped me settle and feel more at one with the house in the early days," she said, before letting out a great bark of a laugh. "Hark at me, admitting such things. I'm hardly your New Age goddess type."

Matt's parents had retired to a bungalow, leaving the newly-weds to run the farm.

"We feel we've done our share now," Rosemary told Rachel. "I know you'll do an excellent job of carrying on in our footsteps."

"No pressure, then," was Kate's joking remark, when Rachel told her, on one of their occasional meet-ups to go round the city centre and what Kate called "proper" shops. She was steadily climbing the promotion ladder, and deservedly so, even though it meant she hadn't had the chance to take up Matt and Rachel's standing invitation to visit them.

Rachel wasn't twiddling her thumbs, either, as she set up and ran the small Bed and Breakfast to bring in some much-needed money to help the farm. It was an obvious solution. Not only did she have the business acumen, but she also loved cooking and baking, and the spacious kitchen was a joy to work in. But the hard winter just past had meant difficult times for both. If only there was a way to expand the business.

"I wonder if we could convert the old milking shed and dairy into holiday cottages?" she suggested to Matt.

"It would be nice to see them being used for something more than storage," he agreed. "Ever since Dad sold the dairy herd to concentrate on sheep farming, it's just been standing there, not doing much. I can't help thinking it would be biting off more than we can chew, though."

Thankfully, the Easter holidays brought the usual surge of visitors, among them the Taylor family. They'd been among the first guests at the farm, and had stayed a couple of times since.

"We all love coming here," Megan Taylor said when Rachel mentioned the idea to them as she brought them some more coffee. "The children practically see you as an honorary auntie. We've just been thinking of starting to take our main summer holidays in the Lakes, too. You can't always rely on the weather, to put it mildly, and Alice and Tom are getting more boisterous as they get bigger, so a cottage would be perfect. They'd have room to run around without annoying other guests or getting under your feet."

Rachel smiled understandingly. The children were well behaved, but she'd noticed their parents having to work harder to keep them occupied when indoors. She glanced out of the window at the old outhouses gradually falling into disrepair across the yard.

"The trouble is, it's a big undertaking, not to mention expensive," she said.

"Maybe, but I've noticed several other farms have taken the plunge and are renting out cottages. This is probably one of the best areas in the country for it." James Taylor got hold of little Tom's hands to stop him playing with the salt and pepper pots. Luckily Jenny, one of the farm cats, trotted into the room, which distracted the children. "I've got an architect friend who could probably advise you. If it's any help, we'd definitely be interested in booking."

As if agreeing with his words, the sun chose that moment to slant through the windows and make the whole room glow.

With the Taylors leaving that day, Rachel was soon busy getting their vacated room cleaned and made up ready for a couple who'd be arriving that evening, although their luggage would arrive in the afternoon, transferred from the previous B and B on the route of their walking holiday. It was almost bedtime by the time she was able to tell Matt about the conversation.

"Maybe it would be worth looking into it further," he agreed. "I think a couple of the locals in the pub rent out cottages. We'll ask them for advice when we go for a drink there tomorrow night." He paused.

"What's wrong?" Rachel asked.

"Sometimes I wonder whether I'm selfish, expecting you to live this sort of life. We both work long hours, and we can't afford designer labels or fancy meals out. It's not exactly fun for you."

Rachel laughed. "I don't care about those. Anyway, I had fun when I was younger."

31

"But not now?" Matt frowned.

"I mean a particular sort of fun. Young-woman-in-the-city fun. I loved it at the time, but nowhere near as deeply as I love you, and what we have here."

Matt didn't say any more. In fact he seemed to go too quiet for Rachel's liking.

The Taylors were as good as their word. Two weeks later, the architect, Andrew, visited, even booking himself and his wife in for a couple of days in the process.

"With the right work, these old buildings would definitely be suitable for two cottages – one for a family, and a smaller one for couples," he enthused. He'd already dealt with similar conversions. "I think you could do well, here."

"What about the cost?" Rachel asked. The locals Matt had mentioned had been generous with advice based on their own experience. They'd also been honest about the difficulties involved.

"The best thing at this stage would be to get some firm builders' estimates, so you know how much you'd be letting yourself in for," said Andrew. "I can recommend someone in the area who's done work for me before."

It was soon arranged that the builder would call round the following Saturday evening, the only time he could make it, in between other jobs.

It was busy time for Matt and Rachel, too. As well as the work on the farm, lighter evenings, plus the time of year popular for weddings and anniversary celebrations, meant bookings were plentiful. Far-flung relatives were as glad as the regular tourists for somewhere comfortable to stay in idyllic surroundings.

There also would be another guest that weekend. Rachel's friend, Kate, had finally been able to visit, insisting that she stay as a paying guest.

"If I wasn't using the room, someone else would have been able to book it," she'd said, when Rachel had protested. "You've got to be realistic when you're running a business."

"Tell me something I don't already know," Rachel had laughed.

"This is heavenly," Kate placed her smart travelling case on the bed in the cosy attic room, before the two friends hugged. "I can see this house has brought out the interior designer in you."

"Hardly any interior design's been needed. Rosemary and David had it perfect." She pointed out of the gabled window, with a flourish. "How's that for a view?"

"Oh, that's spectacular. It is rather isolated here, though, isn't it?"

"That's the whole point. People come here to escape."

"Maybe, but you know me," said Kate. "I'm not sure how long I could manage without towns and shops nearby."

"We have both of those, just not on the scale you're used to. Anyway, I'll leave you to get settled while I check on our meal for tonight. It's simmering on the Rayburn as I speak."

"You mean you have kitchens here, too?" Kate put her hands to her mouth in mock surprise, before they both giggled.

"That's right," said Rachel. "All the better for making proper, home-cooked food."

Later, in Rachel and Matt's private quarters, the three of them made short work of that home-cooked food and caught up with each other's news. Even though Kate and Matt had only met a handful of times, they got on well, so conversation flowed easily. They discussed the possible plans about the cottages and cheered when Kate announced she'd been promoted yet again.

"I believe that calls for a celebratory glass of sloe gin," Matt declared, getting a bottle out of the bottom cupboard of the dresser. "I made this last autumn. There were more bottles, but we went through them at Christmas. We take our festive season seriously in the Lakes, you know. There's nothing quite like it."

"True. This place must take a lot of work, though, and you do seem to be putting yourselves on the line with these cottages," Kate said after they'd clinked glasses. "Does it really mean that much to you?"

After exchanging a glance and a smile with Matt, Rachel reached over and took her friend's hands in her own.

"Yes, it does – and I think it's time you experienced something of the magic for yourself. Tell you what, it's forecast fair for tomorrow. Why don't you and I go up onto the fells together?"

"Seriously? In the sort of shoes I wear? Maybe you shouldn't have had that extra glass just now."

"Don't try to change the subject," Rachel warned her. "We can go into Ambleside first and get you kitted out, and show you what the 'proper' shops are around here. Are you up for it?"

Kate looked doubtful for a moment, then squared her shoulders, as Rachel had suspected she would.

"All right, you're on. Just so long as you promise not to propose to me when we're up there."

"Phew! I bet this keeps you fit," Kate commented the next day, when they paused by a tumbling beck to gaze back down over the valley, spread out like one of the patchwork quilts on the beds in the farmhouse.

The route was busy, with everyone making the most of a sunny spring weekend. Early gorse blazed yellow and sunlight sparkled on water. Walkers moved to one side to make way for each other as they filed up the man-made rocky path designed to reduce erosion from countless pounding feet. Stranger greeted stranger with comments about sleeping well tonight and wishing they'd remembered their sun-block.

Most filtered away after the first main plateau, content to marvel at the view and potter round the pretty tarn before retracing their steps.

"We can turn back here if you like," said Rachel.

Kate, never one to leave a job half done, looked up at the rock towering over them.

"I take it there's a proper path to the top?" she asked.

"Let's put it this way, it's just as well you're in the correct footwear."

That morning's shopping trip had been a revelation. From being reluctant at first, Kate had soon become fascinated by the whole process, delving into the mysteries of "breathable fabrics" and "shock absorbing midsoles".

Even so, it was a stiff climb. The last part was quite a scramble, and they both found their legs were shaking when they reached the summit, but the effort was worth it.

"What a view!" Kate gasped, once they'd got their breath back.

Way below, lakes seemed mere ponds, surrounded by pocket-handkerchief fields and patches of woodland. It was like looking down on a miniature world, a mythical kingdom of their very own.

"Now can you understand why I never want to leave?" asked Rachel.

Kate held up her hands. "I've travelled to many places, but this…"

34

She motioned at the space all around them. "This is something else. I can see why people say they find it inspiring. In fact, it's inspiring me right now." She turned back to face her. "I've had an idea that might help your predicament. How does this sound?"

Rachel's eyes widened as she outlined her proposal.

"Interested?" Kate asked, when she'd finished.

"You bet I am. Wow, you must be pretty high up, to have that much influence."

Kate beamed. "I am. Almost as high as we are, here."

They excitedly discussed various possibilities on the way back to the farm, where the builder, accompanied by a pleasant-looking younger man called Graham, had arrived to assess the work. Rachel noticed Kate's cheeks suddenly seemed flushed when Graham introduced himself. Whether that was from the exertions of the day, or something else, it was difficult to tell.

When she snuggled up with Matt that night, he was as delighted with Kate's suggestion as Rachel had been.

"It's only a temporary, part time contract, promoting the online presence of some of the company's clients," she explained. "I'll need to travel into the office one day a week, but I can do the rest of the work at home. Thank goodness we have a decent broadband connection here."

"I'm glad, and not just about the money," he said.

"What do you mean?"

He took a deep breath. "I don't know. I was worried Kate might still tempt you to go back to the city. Now you can get the best of both worlds."

"There was never any question of me going back, silly. This is the most important place for me. With you," she added, just before their lips met. "And don't you ever forget it."

Nearly a year later, spring had come round again as Rachel welcomed the Taylor family into the cottage they'd booked for Easter.

"You're the first people in here, so I suppose you're sort of my guinea pigs," she told them. "Don't be afraid to be honest about any shortcomings. That way I'll know if any more needs to be done."

"It's perfect." Megan Taylor's eyes sparkled as she looked around. "I can tell that we're going to be happy in here, whatever the weather. The children have already fallen in love with their rooms. It really is like a

35

home from home, only even nicer."

"I hope so. It's already booking well. "

The past year had involved a lot of hard work. To Rachel's eternal gratitude, her mother-in-law, Rosemary had helped, too, insisting she was delighted to be involved.

"I was getting bored in the bungalow. At least David has his vegetable garden to keep him occupied."

Working for Kate's company had certainly come in useful to help finance the bank loan, taking off a lot of the pressure. Not only that, but in many ways the two friends had grown closer than ever, as Kate regularly booked the little attic room.

"It's like having my own little nest to escape to," she said. "You're right. It truly is magical here."

The scenery wasn't the only element that had changed her mind, Rachel suspected, as she waved to Graham, who still called round frequently, even though the building work had been completed. Those walking boots of Kate's were getting plenty of wear, thanks to their long hikes together. Somehow Rachel had a feeling that those two would soon have some decisions to make. There was something purposeful in Graham's expression today, and it didn't surprise her to hear that they were planning a walk among the Langdale Pikes.

"Just so long as he remembers to watch where he kneels when he proposes," Matt joked.

Whether Kate moved here, or Graham moved to the city, was up to them. Whatever plan they agreed on, she hoped they would be as happy as she was with Matt.

She was brought out of her thoughts by little Alice Taylor.

"Auntie Rachel? Are you baking a cake today? Because you promised I could help when you did. Is that all right?"

"Of course it is. How about some fairy cakes?"

As they started to mix the ingredients, she looked out of the kitchen window, to where the mountains watched benignly from the distance. She was glad that her and Matt's children would grow up in what may well be the best place on earth. With their first child due later this year, that was a happy prospect. And if, once grown, the wider world beckoned and they chose to move on, she'd understand.

She knew that the house would understand, too, as she felt its reassurance whenever she placed her palms against its cool stone walls.

36

A Secret Place

Not many people visited the tarn, tucked away as it was behind the trees. It was hardly the most scenic in the Lake District, a poor relation compared with so many of the others that were surrounded by dramatic mountains and the wild beauty of the fells.

Matters weren't helped by the fact that reaching the spot involved several miles' walk along a stony track, through line after line of tall, ruler-straight pines. Even then, it was only found by those who spotted the faint path branching off and took the time to follow it over a small rise, to be rewarded by the water opening out before them like a dream. Yet, for those who did discover the tarn, its tranquillity, with trees and sky reflected perfectly in its mirror-like surface on a calm day, made it a gem in its own right.

It was on such a day when one particular couple approached, their voices breaking into the stillness.

"Hey, Jen, look at this."

The young man's words were unnecessary. Jen was already looking, as they both stopped of one accord.

Both of them, as was the fashion of the time, had long, dark hair and wore flared trousers and large collars. Arguably that wasn't the most suitable clothing for a walk, but worse had been known here. They held hands as they drew closer to the shore, skirting round the boggier stretches and stepping over tussocks of long grass.

"Who'd have thought this would be here?" Jen remarked, blue eyes wide.

"I noticed it on the map this morning, but it seemed too small to be worth bothering with."

"What a thing to say, Richard! You'd better not think that about me." She shoved him playfully. Standing side by side, she reached somewhere between his shoulder and his elbow.

"Of course I don't. And I never will." Silence fell again briefly as they shared a kiss.

"Uh-oh. We've got company." He nodded across the water to where a pair of Canada geese were making their determined way towards them, leaving perfect "V"s in their wake. "Maybe we should have our picnic somewhere else."

"But it's so idyllic here. We're not frightened of a couple of geese."

They found a flat, dry patch, warm in the sun, and started to unwrap their sandwiches. At the appearance of food, the residents made their presence more keenly felt. The meal was punctuated with cries of "Shoo!" and "Go away," with admittedly nervous laughter in between, all the while half-kneeling in preparation for a quick get-away.

Whether the geese were in a mellow mood, or whether they heard Richard's jokes about recipes for roast goose - accompanied by loud tuts from Jen – they limited their aggression to a few hisses. Once the sandwiches were finished, they soon lost interest and swam away, perfect "V"s and all, leaving the couple to bask in the sunshine and talk in peace.

As the afternoon drew on, Richard checked his watch.

"We'd better go. We're supposed to be meeting my parents in Hawkshead at five, remember."

Jen sighed. "Do you think they'll like me?"

"Of course they will. Don't worry, they're not ogres. You'll be fine."

Slowly, they retraced their steps along the path through the trees. At the brow of the rise, where the earth was driest and carpeted with pine needles, they both looked back, taking in the jewel-like water as if to hold the image in their memories.

"I wish we didn't have to leave," said Jen. "It feels like a special, secret place, somehow."

"I know," Richard replied. "Don't worry. We'll come back, some day."

Time moved on. The seasons turned. Autumn colours, resplendent against a deepening blue sky and faithfully reflected by the water, drew appreciative gasps and clicks of cameras.

Come winter, hardly a soul strode the path. In the coldest weather, the tarn froze over with good strong ice, a skater's dream. But while delighted shouts rang out from other frozen tarns in more favoured places, here the silence was broken only by the moan of the wind in the trees, or the crack of twigs where unseen animals foraged for food.

Gradually, the days lengthened and warmed. The Canada geese, constant to the place and to each other, built their nest and prepared to raise their young. More walkers appeared - some returning, some new. But another three summers would pass before the couple from that other day fulfilled their promise.

This time they wore their hair shorter. Their clothes were more practical, corduroy trousers and fleece tops, with picnic and waterproofs packed in a strong rucksack. Walking boots enabled them to stride confidently over ground where they'd previously had to pick their way.

But they no longer walked hand in hand.

After a few minutes they found the same spot as before, spreading a rug for comfort.

Right on cue, the geese charged across the water.

"Oh, great." Richard moaned. "I'd forgotten about them."

"That's not the only thing," his wife retorted

"Look, I've already said I'm sorry about forgetting our anniversary. I'll make it up to you, I promise. It's just that there's been so much going on at school. Then there's everything else to deal with. Bills to pay. Stopping the house from falling down."

"Meetings to attend," Jen added. "Train season ticket to buy. Shopping to pick up on the way home. It's endless for me, as well, you know."

"At least you don't have to worry about trying to control a class and convince them of the relevance of the carbon cycle."

"You should try dealing with some of my clients."

By now, they both knew from experience, they could probably carry on like this for hours.

Jen sighed and plucked a stalk of grass, twirling it between her fingers. "Who'd have thought life would be so complicated? Sometimes I wish we could be like those geese. They have no worries. Just the fun of finding different ways to terrorise innocent picnickers."

"I wouldn't be so sure. There's the small matter of survival for them to contend with. At least we don't have to worry about that." Richard knelt on the rug. "Why are we arguing when we should be spending the afternoon enjoying all this? It's what we came back for, after all."

So that was what they did, letting the sun warm them and the place work its magic, as it had that time before. Even the geese didn't spoil it. "Real" life may have brought more worries, but it had also taught more assertiveness. It probably helped, too, that Richard could throw bread a long way.

When the sun disappearing behind the thick screen of trees told them it was time to go, they paused and looked back.

"We'll try not to leave it so long before we return," said Richard.

Jen said nothing, just nodded as they walked away, holding hands again.

The forests on the slopes below the tarn were "managed forests", a fact evidenced by the regular appearance of Land Rovers along the labyrinthine tracks winding around the hills.

There came a day when lorries lumbered up, to carry away felled trees, leaving swathes of land lying bare, like a scar on the landscape, until new saplings would make their mark.

The tarn, being a special place, was left undisturbed. Sometimes workmen wandered over to it during their break. They'd sit down on the ground or lean against the trunks and look out at the scene, nearly always feeling more content as a result. The geese, wary of the noise of so much machinery, kept their distance.

"They could do with a bench here," one of the men said, on their last visit before moving on to another job. "I'll put in a note about it. You never know, something might get done."

Once the workmen were gone, the birds came back, to build another nest and resume their old patterns. Far away, Richard and Jen were doing their own nest-building. They decorated the spare room, washed and put aside tiny sheets and blankets and, in the evening light when dusk would be creeping over the tarn, read every book on parenthood they could lay their hands on.

They kept their promise, taking a year less to come back this time.

"Oh good, a bench." Richard put the rucksack down on one end. "We can keep Amy out of reach of the geese more easily."

Their appearance had changed again. Jen now had permed hair, as was the current fashion. Richard had followed fashion, too, but the less said about his attempt at a mullet, the better.

Inevitably, the geese approached, long necks craning, but they were no longer so young now, and up against a protective father.

"If you glare down on your pupils like that, you'll have them knuckling down to work and passing their exams in no time," his wife joked.

There had been other changes, too. A jetty protruded several feet out past the water's edge and granted a new vantage point over the tarn. The rushes were taller. The trees were bigger, making the spot feel even more secluded, despite the fact that more walkers visited now, guided by wooden, colour-coded route markers.

Over the following years, the family, increased to four in all, kept coming back, as the children grew in parallel with the saplings and learned to love the place as their parents did.

Then came the day that just two of them returned.

With their now greying hair stylishly cut, and faint lines etched on their weathered faces, their gaze swept across the tarn as they settled on the bench with a sense of homecoming.

On this occasion, out of the well-worn rucksack came not only sandwiches, cake and nectarines, but two plastic wine glasses and a small bottle of a highly respectable *merlot*.

"This is what we always promised ourselves," Richard said as he poured the wine. "Time with each other, while we're young enough to enjoy it."

They clinked glasses, insofar as plastic can be "clinked". "Tap" might be a more appropriate word, but wouldn't really suit the mood.

"Happy anniversary," said Richard.

Jen smiled. "It took years of training for you to remember, but you finally did it."

"I only forgot once," came the indignant reply. "I've remembered every year since then."

"Thanks to a few well-placed hints."

The geese, as ever, put in an appearance, albeit a new pair, taking up the mantle from their predecessors. And with a particular fondness for cake. Thanks to years of teaching ball games to the children, as well as a stint in the local cricket team, Richard's throwing skills were better than ever.

"Remember our first time here?" Jen asked as the birds chased after another piece of Madeira.

Richard nodded. "We said this would be our special place, and

41

that's what it turned out to be." He pointed towards an area of long grass. "There's the spot where we had our first two picnics."

"Feel free to sit over there if you wish. I'm comfortable here, thank you."

A chill laced the air as the sun slid behind the trees, the way it had countless times before, and always would, beyond living memory.

The remains of the meal packed reluctantly away, the couple linked arms and ambled up the path, pausing as usual at the rise to look back.

'I wonder when we'll be here again," said Richard.

"One day," Jen replied. "When we're back from our travels."

The surface of the tarn rippled as if in acknowledgment, but they had already turned away, so didn't notice.

Stillness settled once again, but not for long.

Minutes later, two voices not heard by this place before, trickled like a stream through the trees.

"Are you sure we have time to explore? It's getting on."

"Don't worry. It'll stay light well into the evening. It's not as though we have to rush back for anything. We might as well have a look while we're here."

A young couple emerged into the open, hand in hand. Within seconds, they'd stopped talking, amazed at their discovery. In jeans and trainers, they weren't particularly well equipped for walking, especially in comparison with so many these days. But the weather was kind, so they managed.

"Wow, Debs, just look at this place. Who'd have thought this would be tucked away here?"

Already the Canada geese were racing to make their acquaintance - whether wanted or not - with the newcomers, leaving two perfect "V"s that intersected in their wake.

A Rocky Path

I never really knew how Jake and I came to be best mates, but we were, and had been ever since we met at school when we were eleven.

He was the popular one, always cracking jokes in lessons and making the class laugh. I was the quiet one, plodding along, keeping my head down and getting okay marks that couldn't compete with Jake's. Come to think of it, I couldn't compete with Jake in most things. Yet he was always there for me, always a friend. It makes school life a lot easier when you hang out with the cool one. I'm not sure what he got out of it, but there you are.

Maybe it was a case that opposites attract, because now it seemed to be happening all over again, with Trish. I wasn't sure what she saw in me. I didn't even remember asking her out. She'd just stopped by my desk and started talking one day because she'd noticed I was wearing glasses when I didn't normally. When I admitted I usually wore contact lenses and had lost one of them down the plug hole that morning, she said she wore them, too. I said it was impossible to tell, and we sort of went on from there.

Jake's new girlfriend was nothing like his usual sort, either. When I met her for the first time, you could have knocked me over with a feather. She was so ordinary and quiet and, well, I suppose in some ways a bit like me. I'd have thought his type would be someone like Trish. She and Jake seemed to hit it off straight away when the four us met up one evening. In fact, everyone got along so well, that when Jake suggested a day's hiking in the Lake District, we all agreed.

Trish and I arrived first, driving up in my mother's car, which I'd borrowed for the weekend. We stood in the car park, gazing up at the jagged edges of the Langdale Pikes, stark against the cloudless blue sky.

"Imposing, aren't they?" said Trisha, summing things up succinctly as always. That was probably why she was racing up the Marketing ladder while I stumbled on in Accounts, trying to make everything balance and convince everyone it wasn't boring.

"But it's not," she'd insisted when I'd mentioned how I felt about it. "If you don't do your job properly, the rest of us haven't a leg to stand on."

One of the dictionary definitions of a pike is a point or spike. Looking at their distinctive shape, I had to agree they were aptly named, and was just about to say so when who should come tearing into the car park with a slightly peaky-looking Karen in the passenger seat, but Jake?

He swerved into the space next to ours, and after we'd all said "Hello" and "What an amazing morning", we started to get ready for the trek.

I knew Jake never did things by halves, and that it was important to be properly equipped, but even I was taken by surprise by the sheer amount of gear he had.

"What are you planning to do with all that lot?" I quipped. "Conquer the Matterhorn?"

"Nah." He grinned. "That's next weekend."

Why is the first part of a walk always so deceptively easy? Initially, looking up at what we were about to tackle didn't put me off, mainly because we were walking among trees at this stage and they blocked the view, and we were keeping our heads down most of the time to avoid tripping over roots. Once out of the trees, though, there was no escaping what was ahead. It even shut Jake up for a second.

Desultory chat gave way to the day's business of putting one foot in front of the other, trying not to think about the distance, and saving our breath for the steep rise that went on and on, before the next rise, and the next and the next after that...

After a while we stopped for a breather and looked back. It was gratifying to see how far we'd already come. The valley spread out below us like a blanket. The sun reflected off the tops of cars in the car park as if they were the backs of little beetles.

The sight of a beck hurtling down the slope beside us made me glad I'd brought a bottle of water, because if I got too thirsty that enticingly sparkling water would be sorely tempting. I'd tried some once on a school trip, then wished I hadn't because we brought some back and our biology teacher put a drop under a microscope and made us look. Jake thought it was a great laugh, but it was a wonder I got any sleep that night as I imagined all those microbes wriggling round my insides. And that

44

was before he mentioned the sheep further upstream. Of course, he'd carried on the same as ever, because no-one could tell him what to do, but I'd played it safe from then on.

"What are these sacks of boulders?" Trish asked, pointing to some big canvas bags we kept encountering every so often.

"They're for building up more of the path," Jake explained, before I had a chance to open my mouth. "Encouraging everyone to stick to it stops the ground to each side being eroded."

Some of the boulders had already been put in place, making a giant, very uneven set of steep steps, often slanted, twisting and turning to graduate the ascent, but still hard work despite that. It was one of those paths where every time you get over the next rise you expect to see the top, but all you see are more rises, and the final goal seems as far away as ever. I tried not to think about the fact that once we'd made it, we'd have to come all the way down again.

By the time we stopped for another break, I was already huffing and puffing, and though the others were, too, I was convinced they weren't as loud as me. It was tempting to sit down, but I knew from bitter experience that if we did, it would be that much harder to get up again. We all remained standing, stretching to ease our backs and necks, and trying not to gulp our water down too fast or it would never last the day.

Trish was standing close to me.

"This is all very different from the Midlands, where I come from," she said. "It's flatter there."

"What made you move up here?" I couldn't help asking.

"Pure chance. I saw a job advertised and applied almost on a whim, thinking it would be a useful first step if nothing else. I got it, and here I am. I can't believe almost a year's gone by since then."

"How long are you planning to stay?" I tried to sound casual.

"Well, originally, it was just going to be till something better came along. The funny thing is, I really like it where I am. I love the beauty of this landscape, and I love my flat. In the long run I'd like to have my own business, and buy an old stone farmhouse with views across the hills." She turned to face me. "How about you? What plans do you have?"

I couldn't think of anything to say. My philosophy was to take one day at a time, though Jake was always telling me I should make more of myself.

"Let's get moving," he said, now. "We've still got a long way to

45

go."

I noticed him helping Karen over some of the more difficult sections, being very attentive. She must be pretty special. I was glad. It was time he had someone like that in his life. I'd have liked to offer to help Trish, but there was no point. She was managing very nicely, thank you.

At last we made it to Stickle Tarn, where we settled down and had lunch. As we dropped our rucksacks by the shore, it came to me that we couldn't have planned for a more perfect day. The sun was shining. It was even warm enough for us to have got down to our T-shirts.

Somewhere below us was the rest of the world. We couldn't see it from here, and I for one didn't need to, because this spot was a little universe in itself. The surface of the tarn, undisturbed by the slightest breeze, mirrored the fresh-washed blue of the sky as well as the dark, brooding crag of Pavey Ark, which dominated the skyline and towered over us like a giant rock fist thrust up through the earth.

Hunkering down on sun-warmed stones, swapping sandwiches and different flavoured crisps, we could have been a group of kids on a Scouts' camping trip, not a bunch of twentysomethings hauling their way up the career ladder. Every so often one of us would go to the edge of the tarn and dip a hand in the icy, clear water.

All we had to contend with now was the climb down. That wasn't a worry. Having set off good and early, we could take it nice and slowly, and still have time for a well-earned pint in the pub at the bottom.

I was fondly imagining the scene, when Jake stood up.

"Right."

Something purposeful about the way he said that made me uneasy. Why was he looking up so intently at that jagged edge above us, when nearly all the other walkers who had turned up seemed happy to potter round the tarn before turning back?

I soon found out.

"We're going up there."

"You must be joking," I protested. "We planned a day's walking, not mountaineering."

"We're not going vertically, pea-brain! Well, not quite." He produced an Ordnance Survey map from his state of the art rucksack. "There's a path that goes round by the side and works its way to the top. We've got this far. We might as well finish the job as we've got such

46

perfect conditions."

I glanced at the others for their reaction. Trish nodded. After a second's hesitation, so did Karen.

"So the route's okay, then?" I asked. "Basically more of what we've been doing so far?"

"Pretty much. Or not much harder, and only for a few bits. You'll be fine."

The first part of the path was pleasant enough, curving round to the side of the rock and inviting us on. It was easy to forget that logically, looking at what was before us, that would have to change at some stage. Sure enough, the way got steeper and steeper.

"Remind me never to believe you again," I called out to Jake with what remnants of breath I had in my body as I scrabbled up a practically vertical section of rock.

"Don't worry. It's not much further," he called back.

He and Trish were several yards ahead, making it look ridiculously easy. Karen was a couple of feet ahead of me, not saying anything, while I brought up the rear.

As ever, Jake had stretched the truth. It was much further. By the time we finally reached the summit, I seriously believed my legs wouldn't push me up another single rock. All I wanted to do was collapse on the ground and feel the springy, sheep-cropped turf beneath me.

So I did, and it was so good, as comfortable as any mattress. There was nothing between me and the sky.

Then there was the view.

When we peered over the edge, the tarn, directly below, looked surreal, as if someone had cut out a piece of dark blue shiny paper and stuck it on a wind-bleached, pale brown background. Distant settlements were like tiny pebbles scattered at random. Coniston Water and Windermere were both clearly visible, while Grasmere and Rydal Water seemed like puddles. A tractor in a distant field, far below, made me think of an insect crawling over cloth.

"Aren't you glad I dragged you up here?" Jake asked.

"All right," I admitted. "I am."

After we'd rested, we started off on the return journey, taking an easier route down the other side of the rock so as to rejoin the path round the tarn. Part of me wasn't surprised when Jake and Trish pulled ahead of us again. They were chatting in a carefree manner, striding on as if the path was as smooth as a road.

"They're like a pair of mountain goats, aren't they?" said Karen, taking me by surprise. She'd hardly spoken to me up till now.

"They are," I agreed. "Still, there's no point in us risking our necks. We'll take our own time. They've got to wait for us at some stage."

We managed to catch up with them by using a crafty short cut, picking a route between small boulders and getting down on our backsides to navigate some scree, having a laugh in the process.

Jake stood, arms folded, as he watched us approach.

"Have you any seat left in those trousers, after that?" he snapped.

"Oh, I think there's a wear or two left in them yet," I fired back, surprised. "I'm sure you'll tell me when there isn't."

Normally he'd have taken that as a cue to crack a joke or two, but he seemed in a bad mood, so we just pushed on.

When we arrived at the giant rock-step path we'd come up earlier, it seemed longer than ever. The only thing that kept me going was the thought of the pint I'd sink when we got to the pub. I could almost taste it.

Jake and Trish charged off again. Soon we could see just the occasional bobbing of their heads, when the gaps between the rocks allowed. After a little longer, we couldn't even even see that.

"You and Jake have known each other a long time, haven't you?" Karen asked, as we negotiated a near-ninety-degree turn in the path.

"Since we were eleven," I replied.

"In that case, can you explain why he always seems to be holding something back, even though he's so talkative a lot of the time?"

That put me in a quandary. Was it was my place to tell her what had happened in Jake's life? Yet, in some ways, didn't Karen deserve to know? She'd come through today without making a single complaint, and the fact she was asking the question said a lot, while I had the distinct impression he really liked her. At least, to the extent he'd let himself.

I took a deep breath and, as we picked our way down, leaning on rocks and slopes to help keep our balance, told her about him losing his dad when he was fourteen, and how since then he'd always pushed himself and built up barriers so he'd never have to know loss like that again.

"My life's been very ordinary, so I don't know much about these things, but I'm sure there must be better ways of coping," I concluded.

48

Then Karen told me her story, how she'd caught her long-term boyfriend with her best friend when he was supposed to be away with relatives.

"It took me more than two years to feel ready to trust again, so I know what it's like to need to stay in a shell. At first, I couldn't understand how someone like Jake could see anything in someone like me – after all, I'm not the high-flying type. But since I've spent more time with him, I can't help thinking there's more to him under that smooth surface than meets the eye. Like there's more under that tarn up there than you'd realise from walking round it."

While she was talking, something else was beginning to bother me. For a while now there hadn't been so much as a glimpse of the other two. It occurred to me that, as the day had progressed, he and Trish seemed to have been getting along better and better.

"Gavin! Karen!"

My broodings were interrupted when Trish came into view. Her face was red from exertion.

"Jake's slipped," she gasped. "He's hurt his ankle. I'm not sure how badly, but he's swearing enough for the sheep to keep their distance. He wouldn't let me call Mountain Rescue. Reckons we should be able to get him back between us, as it's not far."

This time it was Karen and me who were in front, still being careful since we didn't want another of us coming a cropper, but with a sense of purpose urging us on.

"I kept telling him to slow down," Trish said, as she got her breath back. "He wouldn't listen. Typical, pig-headed male."

"How bad's the swelling?" I asked.

"It was coming up pretty fast. I dunked my sweatshirt in the beck to make a cold compress. That seemed to help."

When we reached Jake, a few minutes later, he was sitting by the side of the path, grimacing with pain.

"You idiot," I couldn't resist saying.

"Idiot yourself," was all the reply he could muster as I lifted off the compress.

Trish had done good job. His ankle was swollen, but not as badly as it could have been.

"Well, Speedy Gonzalez, your mega-boots have probably saved you. It doesn't look like anything's broken, but we'd better get you

49

checked."

He groaned. "Saturday night in A and E? You know much I hate hospitals. Can't we at least go to the pub first? It's only down there."

He nodded down to the valley, and I have to say I felt for him. The place was tantalisingly close and so inviting.

"Not if you're going to hospital." Karen's voice was firm. "We need to get you an X-Ray first. Only then can you have a drink."

She was right, of course. But all this talk of drink reminded me that my own throat was incredibly dry, and my water bottle empty. The beck was right next to us, sparkling in the afternoon sun. It was no good. I stepped across, cupped some in my hands and took a drink.

Jake managed a grin. "You do realise there are sheep, further up?"

He ducked as I threw my plastic bottle at him.

With the help of some other passing walkers, we managed to half support, half carry him the rest of the way. Over seven hours had passed since we'd set off.

It was Karen who came up with the transport logistics.

"I'll drive him," she said. "You two go and relax."

"You don't have to," Jake told her. "You can stay here, if you like. I can sort out a taxi."

He glanced at me, and suddenly I realised the reason for his apparent bad mood earlier. He'd been making the same assumptions about Karen and me as I'd started to about him and Trish. The difference was that he was being more generous about it.

Not that it mattered. Karen wasn't one to give in so easily.

"You need a friend with you, and I know the way."

"My car's quite, er, lively. Not exactly your usual little runaround," Jake said.

She smiled sweetly. "That's not a problem. My dad taught me to drive. Did I ever mention he used to be a rally driver?"

Jake's mouth was still wide open as they roared off, with Karen well and truly at the wheel.

The evening sun bathed the surrounding fells in a golden glow as Trish and I sat down with our drinks outside the pub. Around us, other tired but contented walkers talked quietly or simply soaked up the atmosphere.

"Isn't it amazing here?" Trish said after a while, breaking into our pensive silence.

I nodded. "It's like that in all the valleys, or dales. Langdale, Eskdale, Wasdale – they've each got their own character."

"You seem to know a lot about it."

"I always used to come up here with my parents. I've loved it for as long as I can remember."

In a field on one of the slopes, sheep were running over to the farmer bringing their feed on a trailer. A few yards away from us, chaffinches hopped round the bird table, or between benches, looking for crumbs. A springer spaniel, worn out from a day on the fells with his owners, watched them lazily.

"I wonder if Jake's been sorted out yet?"

"It depends how busy they are at the hospital," I said. "Somehow I've got a feeling Karen won't stand for too long a wait."

Trish looked thoughtful. "It's funny, isn't it, when she was so quiet for the rest of the day? Then again, I never really got round to talking to her. I suppose you got to know her better."

"Yeah, well. You went on ahead with Jake, didn't you?" I couldn't resist pointing out. "Why was that?"

She took a long draught from her cider. "I'm not sure. I sort of did it without thinking. I suppose my competitive streak makes me so used to wanting to keep up, it becomes a habit. Today's made me wonder whether that's always the best thing to do."

"Because you might end up with a broken ankle?"

"Because I've come to realise that some things are more important." She cleared her throat. "So...Every dale has its own character, does it? Do you reckon you could introduce me to them?"

"I could. I warn you, it might take some time."

"Oh, I can be patient when I have to. Don't get me wrong, though. I'll still be the same as ever at work. I want that stone farmhouse."

That was fine by me. I wouldn't have her any other way.

For my part, maybe it was time for me to be a little more assertive, instead of holding back. Still, I might go back to being careful about what water I drank.

City Girl, Country Girl

Jo rubbed her head where she'd bumped it yet again on the sloping ceiling of the tiny porch, and wondered how she'd ever thought her little house's quirks so endearing.

Its solid stone walls were permanently cold to the touch, the small windows always made it seem dark inside, and the porch where she kept her waterproofs and walking boots still caught her out, as it had just now, even after two years.

The boots and waterproofs were essential to anyone living around here, of course, and had been part of her life, in various sizes and colours, for as long as she could remember. Her father, a keen walker, had always made a point of living no more than an hour's drive away from the Lake District. As soon as Jo had been old enough to accompany him, he'd introduced her to the gentler routes, gradually progressing to the more challenging fells.

Not surprisingly, she'd grown up to love the place as much as he did. So when a suitable job had come up in the area, she'd jumped at the chance. A great-aunt leaving her a useful legacy, and parents also willing to help out towards the deposit on a terraced house just outside the National Park, led to the conclusion that all the omens were pointing in one direction, and that was the direction she took.

"What if you feel different after a while?" her friend, Melissa, had warned. "You might find you're stuck, all the way out there."

Jo didn't listen, hankering for the wide open spaces and ever-changing nature of the mountains.

Now, though, she found even the most beautiful surroundings could lose their charm when she ended up in traffic jams at tourist bottlenecks on her way home from work, often with her car's windscreen wipers going at full pelt. Goodness only knew where Wordsworth had got his idea about wandering lonely as a cloud. Clouds always had plenty of company so far as she could see - each other! Unlike her.

It was different from the days when she'd shared a house with her old university friends. There'd always be someone to talk to, or go out to the theatre or cinema with. Here, she hardly seemed to know anyone her own age. Perhaps the time was right to move back to the Smoke, admit that the Lake District was just for holidays. Yet something always stopped her.

"It's up to you," was her dad's reaction when she phoned him to talk about it. "Personally, if I'd ever moved to the Lakes, wild horses wouldn't drag me away, but reality can be different from the dream. Just remember, if you do go back, you won't be able to change your mind. Chances of a lifetime are called that for a good reason."

It was the fourth morning in a row that Melissa hadn't been able to get a seat on the bus. To add insult to injury, the bus company had just announced another fare increase.

Not that she should be complaining, she supposed. She had a job slap bang in the centre of the very same city where she had so enjoyed being a student. Wasn't that what she'd always aimed for?

Coming from a small backwater in the middle of nowhere, Melissa had dreamed of city lights and glamour. She'd loved the big name department stores, with masses of space devoted to her favourite cosmetics, and assistants practically queueing up to offer free makeovers. The only drawback was that she was always tempted to buy some of the products afterwards, and they cost more than she could afford. In true Melissa style, she had soon overcome that hurdle by getting a part-time job on one of the counters she'd enjoyed frequenting. It turned out to be an advantage in more ways than one. To her astonishment, after finishing her degree, she'd been taken on as a management trainee at the same store.

"Your experience and enthusiasm shone through," she was told later.

Melissa didn't feel so enthusiastic now, swept along by the stream of commuters all heading for their allotted places of work. The tall glass and concrete towers looked dismal in the never-ending rain. The best word to describe the appearance of the old cathedral that usually stood so proud was "dispirited". Even the fountains in the square were a dull, uniform grey, with no sunlight to sparkle through them and make rainbows.

"Practically anywhere looks miserable in this weather," Helen, her boss, said over coffee during their break. "If you'd done what your family expected, right now you'd be teaching in a small town school classroom full of damp children." She put on a mock-thoughtful expression. "Aroma of damp clothes, or the latest fragrance from Chanel? Hmmm. Difficult choice."

Melissa laughed, yet she still felt restless. Who'd have thought she'd grow bored of city life? While it used to be fun sharing a house with friends, changes over the last couple of years meant it just wasn't the same any more. Jo had left, for instance, even though everyone had said she was mad at the time.

Lately, she'd taken to reading lifestyle magazines instead of her usual fashion glossies. She liked looking through them last thing at night, in bed with cup of herbal tea. Along with the features on how people had renovated cosy cottages with various "finds", her favourite sections were those interviewing women who'd set up their own businesses. Home-made scented soaps and oils featured frequently. So far as Melissa could gather, they didn't seem that difficult to make, and with her sales and marketing training, she might be build up a nice little business of her own. Then there'd been that very tempting episode of *Escape to the Country* she'd happened to catch, last Sunday, when she hadn't felt like going out anywhere.

It would be a huge gamble, and she'd still need a job to support herself. Still, it was worth looking into. Jo had taken the plunge. She might have some good advice.

As it happened, nearly a hundred miles away, Jo was sitting by her little stone fireplace, flicking through a fashion magazine she'd picked up on a whim in the small local supermarket. She couldn't remember when she'd last bought one of these. It made her quite nostalgic for former days when she and Melissa used to go round the city centre shops together. Of course, Mel was still there and, knowing her, still shopping till she dropped. Perhaps she was the best person to help her arrive at a decision. In fact, now she came to think of it, it was a while since they'd had a really good natter on the phone, as opposed to exchanging texts.

Before she could change her mind, Jo was dialling her old friend's number.

"Well, well, well. So the wanderer returns. What happened? Did the sheep suddenly stop talking to you? "

"Very funny, Richard," Jo retorted. "I see your so-called sense of humour hasn't changed."

"Ouch, that hurt." Richard put a hand to his heart. "Welcome back, anyway. It's good to see you."

Jo smiled her thanks as she picked up her case and headed for the stairs. It had been an inspired suggestion of Mel's that they should try a "house swap" for a few days to help them work out what they really wanted. Three weeks after their phone conversation, here she was, in her old shared house. It felt strange coming back. She was glad that at least one of the original housemates was still in residence.

"Mel still has the same room," Richard told her. "Up in the clouds. You might need an oxygen mask. Someone else rents your old room. We don't see her much. She works nights."

"Yes, Mel told me. Do you fancy a drink, later?"

Richard grimaced. "I would, but I've got an early start at work, which will mean setting off even earlier to beat the rush hour. It's not just you country folk who get up at the crack of dawn, you know."

Jo swallowed her disappointment and managed to grin. "Never mind. An early night will probably do me good. I'd forgotten how busy the motorway gets the further south you come. Anyway, I intend to put in a full day tomorrow."

Later, just before she settled down for the night, Jo opened the attic window to gaze out at the lights stretching to the horizon and listen to the hum of traffic.

"The city never sleeps," she murmured to herself, "but I'm going to."

As she crawled under the duvet and settled down, she thought dreamily of all that life, going on outside.

Up in the Lake District, as Jo's neighbour, Mary, showed her in, Melissa had to admit to herself that she'd been expecting something more... *Cumbrian*. The restful sound of a nearby beck fresh from the mountains, perhaps, or even the odd sheep turning up for a little look, though it would have to find its way out of its field or fell, or wherever sheep lived, and trot along the pavement.

"There's a handy little supermarket just round the corner," said Mary, bringing her back to reality. "Jo told me to tell you she's left the fridge well stocked."

A fridge that didn't have to be shared? Wonderful!

"She also said to remind you there are some spare blankets in the cupboard. It can get cold here at night. Now, do let me know if there's anything you need. I'm only next door."

Later that evening, Melissa could hardly believe how time had flown. She'd been so comfortable sitting by the proper fireplace in the little sitting room. After a while she even switched off the television and listened to the ticking of the clock.

"Well," she said to the stillness. "I suppose I'd better turn in. I've got a long day ahead of me tomorrow if I want to do all the things I've been planning."

Upstairs, she parted the curtains and peered outside. Beyond the edge of the little town, everything was a dark, dark blue, almost black.

Wow, she thought. All that empty space!

"How are you finding the big, bad city?" Melissa asked Jo on the phone, the following evening.

"Great," Jo answered. "Or it was, once I'd battled my way in and managed to find a parking space."

"If you think that's bad, you should try the public transport. It's like playing sardines, without any birthday cake afterwards. Come on, tell me about the rest. Which shops did you go to?"

"Loads. Oh, Mel, I'd forgotten what it was like to spend a day going round a warm, comfortable shopping centre and still have more to see at the end of it. I treated myself to some new clothes and I've even booked a ticket for a play tonight. It's got the lead actor from that series we were talking about." She named the one she meant. "I suppose you've already seen it?"

"To be honest, I haven't been keeping up with these things, recently," Melissa admitted. "Still, if he's in, I'll definitely check it out. My day was very revealing," she continued, and went on to describe how, after picking up the hire car, she'd visited one of the local market towns, plus a couple of villages, exploring craft and gift shops. "Obviously, they prefer local products, but I could make soaps and candles infused with blended aromatherapy oils, and labelled with their specific properties – calming, uplifting and so on. I bet there'd be a gap in the market."

"Possibly," said Jo. "If you want to part customers from their money, I suspect you'll need a Lakeland theme. 'Coniston Calm', perhaps?

57

Or 'Windermere Wonder'? I wouldn't really know, mind. I seem to spend all my time sorting out claims for farmers losing their tractors down ditches, or walkers dropping their mobile phones down scree slopes."

"Well, I'm pretty sure I do know." Melissa couldn't help feeling slightly nettled at what she saw as her friend's lukewarm response. "Maybe it's the freshness of the air up here, but I've got a good feeling about this. Tomorrow I'll go round the gift shops in poets' houses and visitor centres, to check out the opportunities there."

Both went quiet for a moment, as if they'd run out of things to say. True to form, it was Melissa who was the first to restart the conversation. That had always been the trouble with Jo, she thought. She had a tendency to sit back and ruminate.

"What are your plans for the next two days?"

"Well, I noticed a massive branch of my favourite chain of bookstores, so I'll happily lose myself in there for a few hours. Then there are a couple of art galleries I'd like to visit. All in all, it looks as if we're both in for a busy time."

That was true, yet not quite in the way either of them had expected.

Jo felt deliciously self-indulgent and spoilt for choice as she browsed through paperbacks in the plush interior of the bookshop. She enjoyed the theatre trip, too. There was a whole range of films and plays available for her to see, not to mention one of her favourite groups performing at a local venue.

But it would have been so much nicer if there'd been someone to go with. Everyone in the house always seemed to be either on their way out or just coming in and about to collapse in their rooms. At home, the neighbours were always ready to chat, as were the farmers she saw in her job working for an insurance company, even if they did usually grumble about everything, and insisted on serving her mugs of tea strong enough to stand a spoon in.

Then there were the shops themselves. At first, she'd been impressed by the huge range on offer, and treated herself to a few things she'd been saving for, but a lot of the clothes simply weren't practical for her day-to-day life. And everywhere was crowded.

At least she found one of the art galleries she wanted to visit, larger than any of those she frequented in the Lakes. The moment she walked into its hushed stillness, she finally knew a sense of calm. Not the same calm as the fells and valleys, obviously, but calm nevertheless.

As if by some twist of fate, she came upon a painting of a scene she knew and loved : Great Gable, as seen across the brooding surface of Wastwater. Its symmetrical, imperious outline seemed to look back at her so intently, the pull was almost physical.

"No wonder there are so many poets and thinkers in the Lakes," Melissa said, when they chatted again, a couple of days later. "There's nothing else to do. I went round the gift shops, but they don't seem that interested in the products I'm thinking of, apart from the odd few here and there." She sighed. "I'm beginning to wonder whether that means a gap in the market or lack of demand. Customers seem mainly to want mint cake, gingerbread, tea towels and warm tops. I even ended up buying a fridge magnet of a sheep. Then there's the fact that everywhere is so spread out. Your petrol bill must be horrendous."

"That's why I've got a small car," Jo replied. "It's economical, yet feisty enough to tackle the mountain passes, as well as compact enough to get by on some of the lanes."

"Assuming you're crazy enough to want to do all that," was her friend's reaction. "And those mountains are decidedly creepy at night. You can almost feel them out there in the dark, looming over everything."

"Do you know what you are?" said Jo. "A Johnny Town-Mouse."

"As in the Beatrix Potter story, where he goes to the country and really hates it? That makes you the other one, who goes to the town. What was his name?"

"Timmie Willie. He was glad to get home, too, just as I'll be. The story's even set in the Lake District."

"So I'm Johnny and you're Timmie?" Melissa giggled. "We'll have to remind each other of that, the next time either of us get itchy feet and start making crazy plans. I'll definitely be glad to get back to civilisation, even if the buses are crowded. And proper, covered shopping centres where you can stay warm and dry. Bliss!"

It was bliss indeed for Melissa to come home. She heaved a sigh of relief as she stepped off the train. Even the sight of the city skyline as it neared its destination had set her pulse quickening. She paused for a moment to savour the scene of everyone bustling about with a sense of purpose beneath the mix of grand Victorian and modern architecture.

59

The thought of the Monday morning "crush hour" still filled her with dread, but she was determined to sort that out. It was time she moved out of the shared house to somewhere nearer the centre. Richard was the only one of their original group still living there, and he'd mentioned something about moving out due to relocating with his job. A new place would cost more, even for something hardly bigger than a broom cupboard, but the savings in travelling costs might help make up the difference. She'd manage it, somehow.

First things first, though. Her number one priority was a latte and maybe even celebratory muffin from her favourite coffee chain. How she'd missed those! Next, she just had time to go shopping for a pair of glamorous shoes so she could get changed out of these sensible monstrosities.

As Melissa walked out onto the street, buildings towering above her, she felt well and truly glad to be back.

Jo's spirits rose even as she drove up the motorway and spotted those same mountains that her friend had complained about, blue in the distance, as if they were old friends waiting to welcome her home.

Of course, she needed more friends of her own age. It was up to her, she realised now, to make the effort to get out and meet people. She'd already decided to join a walking club, as well as start going to one of the little theatres dotted around the district.

While it was true that the house was cold, there was such a thing as insulation. And those dark rooms? Nothing a few tins of paint and some lighter coloured curtains couldn't solve, judging from the tips she'd read in the magazines on Melissa's bedside table.

She just had to remember to mind her head in that porch.

Lakeland Romantics

Edward lay back on the springy turf and concluded there could be nothing better than a Lakeland hillside on a sunny day. Even with his eyes closed, he could picture the mountains and crags, with the china blue sky perfectly reflected in the lake below. No wonder Wordsworth, Coleridge and the other great poets of the age revered the place.

"Gyp! Get back here."

Excited barking shattered his musings. He barely managed to sit up before a black and white dog knocked him down again, adding insult to injury by licking his face. Apparently satisfied, the "Gyp" creature stayed by him, bushy tail waving, to await his owner.

And what an interesting surprise the owner turned out to be.

"Gyp, you bad dog. I hope you're not hurt, sir?"

Edward scrambled to his feet to meet the gaze of a pair of green eyes that glinted with amusement. At the same time, he felt the strangest tingle surge through him, as though from some chemical reaction in one of the many experiments he was always reading about. He tried to see if the newcomer's face betrayed any corresponding sensation on her part, but she seemed more intent on stroking her dog, her long hair falling forward over her shoulders.

"Not at all," he said, "though I must admit he gave me a fright."

The young woman threw back her head and laughed. "That's what you get for lying there, dreaming. Sometimes that's all you visitors seem to do."

"That's because we *are* visitors. Unlike you, we are not fortunate enough to live in a place surrounded by such magnificent scenery."

His indignant response provoked another peal of laughter. "You wouldn't say that if you had to traipse after sheep over the fells when the mist comes down and chills you to the bone." She nodded at the book he was holding. "What's that you're reading?"

"Wordsworth's *Guide to the Lakes*," Edward replied, glad to be back on safer territory.

"Oh, I've heard of him and his set. A right rum lot, they are, if half the things said about them are true."

"But the poetry is wonderful, don't you agree?"

"I wouldn't know. I can't read. I know the names of all these mountains, though," she added, with a stubborn tilt of her chin.

They both gazed across the valley to where the self-same mountains were picked out in all their detail by the sun.

"Well, it's time I was moving," she said. "There's not many of us can do nowt all day."

He couldn't let this vision disappear so soon. "Please - what's your name?"

"Grace Porter." She looked at him curiously. "What's yours?"

"Edward Barnes." An idea came to him as she made to go. "Grace, if I teach you how to read, will you teach me the names of the mountains?"

"I can do. I'll see you here at the same time tomorrow."

It was only as she ran down the slope, with Gyp scampering round her heels, that Edward noticed she was carrying a shepherd's crook.

"Me? A shepherdess?" was her amused reaction, when he asked her the next day. "I suppose I am in some ways. My family are sheep farmers, and I do my bit to help, along with my sister and brothers. It's hard work, but I'd rather do that than toil at the bobbin mills or go into service."

They sat down together on the grass. Edward read to her, tracing a line under the text with his finger as he went. Every now and then he stopped to point out words that matched, spelling out the letters to demonstrate how they worked together.

"Never mind that," Grace interrupted after a while. "Just carry on reading. I like how it sounds, even if it is all fanciful."

It was hardly the image he'd built up in his mind, of her following every word and diligently repeating them to set them in her memory. After noticing her trying to stifle yet another yawn, he decided there was nothing further to be achieved that day and snapped the book shut.

"I think it is time for you to be the teacher, and I the pupil," he said.

Soon his companion was pointing out the fells as casually as if they were neighbouring villages rather than miracles of nature.

"They look well enough today," she warned, "but sometimes they can be dark and angry. Other times you can't see them at all, just feel them watching you as if knowing everything you do. Not that I mind. They're company."

"Now who's being fanciful?" Edward teased.

Over the next week, she told him more about the surrounding area and its people in a matter of fact way that, for Edward, had a charm of its own. Or was that because he was charmed by everything she said and did?

As the profile and character of the landscape became more familiar to him, so too did Grace. It became difficult to imagine passing a single day without her. That day soon came, though, when driving rain and impenetrable mist not only blotted out the hills from view, but made it impossible to think of walking over the field, never mind sitting and reading there.

Instead, Edward spent the day in his lodgings, writing letters that were long overdue. Only when a feeble sun broke through in the late afternoon did he venture out to the post, glad of the opportunity to stretch his legs and take in some fresh air.

The newly moistened grass glowed in the pale light like a scene from a fairy tale. Edward was entranced – until he looked up the steep slope to the higher fields.

There, in the distance, he saw a man and a woman. It was difficult to tell from here, but he was certain that the woman was Grace. She wore the same cloak, had the same dark hair and moved in the same, no-nonsense way. The couple seemed at ease with each other. Was she ever like that with him?

After a few minutes, they walked out of sight through a gap in one of the dry-stone walls that criss-crossed the fells. Edward shuffled back to his lodgings, knowing for the first time what all the poets meant when they wrote of a heavy heart.

"Who were you with yesterday?"

He knew it was impertinent of him to ask, but the question had plagued him all night.

If Grace was offended, she didn't show it.

"That would have been Dan Thwaite, from over the rise. He often passes this way to get to his flock. You could have walked with us, if you'd been there. I told you we have to be out in all weathers."

While Edward bridled at the inference that he was somehow a lesser creature for staying indoors, another matter needled him more.

"Do you know this Dan well?"

"Since we were children." She twirled around as if restless. "Let's not read today. I'd rather walk."

He couldn't help linking her lack of enthusiasm with Dan, even though he knew full well that she often didn't concentrate properly during their reading sessions. Still, it was too cold and damp to sit down, and hadn't he come to the Lake District to be inspired by the landscape in all its moods? It was certainly in a different mood today. The rain may have moved on, but the fells crouched sullenly under a heavy sky.

As the summer drew on, the pair got into the habit of alternately walking and reading, though the former gradually took over from the latter, and Edward became lean and healthy from all the exercise.

Sometimes their path would cross with that of Dan's. The man was pleasant enough, always stopping to exchange a few sentences, but Edward couldn't fail to notice his muscular forearms and firm, set, jaw. Or the way his dark grey eyes softened whenever they settled on Grace.

They drank from mountain streams, or becks, as Grace called them. The water was clear and icy, so unlike that of his home town, to which he must soon return, however much he may try to push the thought to the back of his mind.

Sure enough, as the shadows lengthened, his father wrote to say it was time to stop dreaming, and join his brother in the legal profession.

"Come back with me," Edward begged Grace, when he broke the news of his impending departure. "We can be married. My family will object at first, but they'll soon change their minds. These hands of yours will be rough no more." He held them in his own. "They'll be as soft and smooth as mine," he added, laughing. She had often teased him on the subject.

To his dismay, her eyes filled with tears. She dashed her hand across her face and turned away.

"I'm sorry. I can never leave this place, even for you," she said, after what seemed an age.

"You can see other places..." he began, but she wouldn't let him finish.

"No, I can't. I won't. How can I make you understand? Think of the daffodils you read to me about from those poems. Left in their proper place, they'll flower year after year. Take them away, and after a while they'll flower no more."

64

"Not if they're carefully transplanted."

"The bright ones, grown for your fine, tame gardens, maybe. But the wild ones, that are found here every spring..." she pointed to a slope behind the church. "They don't belong anywhere else."

"I'll write," he said. "I'll never give up hope."

"I won't be able to read your letters, even after all your patience. Or reply to them."

"But you'll know they're from me, and that I'm thinking of you."

That winter was long and hard, the town drab and dismal. When snow came, it brightened the streets only briefly before turning to slush, through which both horses and people floundered. Edward wondered how Grace and her family were managing, so many miles away, looking after the sheep through the worst of the storms. And what the mountains must look like, cloaked in brilliant white.

He worked conscientiously enough at the position his father had obtained for him, but he hated every minute. The times he came closest to being contented were when reading, and when visiting his sister, Marianne, and her children. Robert, at four the eldest, constantly pestered Edward to read to him, a request he was only too happy to oblige. It wasn't long before he was helping the boy to pick out words for himself. Not only that, but he listened, rapt, as Edward told him all about a faraway magical land of lakes and mountains.

"You're a miracle worker," Marianne said one evening, after a tired but happy Robert had been packed off to bed. "No-one else has got him so interested in the written word. You should be a schoolmaster."

All this time, true to his word, Edward sent letter after letter.

True to Grace's word, there were no replies.

At long last, lighter days heralded the arrival of spring. It was on such a day that he received a small parcel. Inside, wrapped in wool, nestled a solitary daffodil, its tight bud just unfurling to reveal the delicate colour within, that declared its origin.

He knew then what he was meant to do.

The weather was fine and mild on his arrival. Edward sent the carriage ahead with his luggage and walked the last mile, both to savour the sensation of being back, and in the hope of calming his nerves.

Although most of the daffodils had finished flowering by now, a few late blooms still lingered on in shady groves. He marvelled at the way everything seemed so vivid. The ground beneath his feet felt firmer, the air clearer, the colours new-washed.

"There you are, Mr Barnes!"

The housekeeper from his lodgings, dressed in what appeared to be her best clothes, bustled towards him.

"I won't be in for the next hour or so, as I'm off to the church for the wedding," she said. "But the house is open. Just go in and make yourself comfortable. There's food on the table if you're hungry."

"Wedding, Mrs Shaw? Who's getting married?"

"Why, Mr Thwaite and Miss Porter, of course. Half the village is there. It'll be a grand celebration. Why don't you come along?"

Suddenly the ground no longer felt so firm. His power of speech deserted him. It was all he could do to shake his head.

"I suppose you must be tired after your long journey," said Mrs Shaw. "You go and rest. I'll pass on your good wishes to the happy couple."

Edward didn't know how long he dozed, or even how he had made it to the deserted house and up the stairs, but when he woke the light was fading and the air had grown chill. That was nothing, compared to the chill inside him, he thought bitterly. For all his book-learning, all his poetry, he was ignorant about life and everything that mattered. The daffodil he had assumed to be a token of Grace's feelings had really, he could see now, been a reminder of where she belonged. And that wasn't with him.

Still only half awake, he thought he heard voices, then rapid footsteps on the stairs, followed by a knock at the door. The next thing he knew, Grace stood before him, looking even more beautiful than he remembered.

He scrambled to his feet.

"Miss Porter. I gather congratulations are in order," he managed to say.

"Indeed they are. This is the happiest day of my life."

How could she say that? How could her eyes sparkle and her lips twitch, when they were only inches away from each other and yet the distance between them was insurmountable?

"I received your letters," she carried on. "They looked very fine.

66

I'm sorry I couldn't read them properly."

"I received your parcel." He felt a lump grow in his throat. "Not that it matters now. I'm sorry, too. I should have realised that we could never be together."

Grace frowned. The spark in her eyes died as she put a hand to her throat and stepped back.

"You mean I'm not welcome here?"

When Edward said nothing, she drew back her shoulders.

"Very well. In that case, I had better take your leave. The dancing will start soon, and everyone will wonder where I am."

It was only as she reached the door that he found it in himself to say the words he knew, as a gentleman and a friend, he ought to say.

"I wish you and your husband a long and happy life together."

She turned. "My husband?" Confound the woman. Her lips were twitching again. "You mean you didn't know?"

"If I did, would I have come back to ask you to marry me? My circumstances have changed," he continued. "I've obtained a schoolmaster's post not far from here, so that you wouldn't have to leave. It's what I want. Even my father relented when he realised the legal profession was not for me. But it's all pointless now."

Maybe he was still asleep, because suddenly he was having the most wonderful dream, where Grace threw her arms around his neck and covered his face in the sweetest kisses.

"I am not married," she laughed. "My sister is."

"But you said this was the happiest day of your life."

"It was, seeing Dan and Martha joined together, and then hearing from old Mrs Shaw that you had returned. But just now, when you said…" She laughed again.

Surely all of that could only ever happen in a dream?

Yet, when she led him downstairs and outdoors, saying he must join in the dancing, the cold evening air convinced him he was awake, after all, and possibly the most fortunate man alive – though Dan might say he had his own claim on that title.

The best thing of all was, as he looked across the lake at the mountains silhouetted against the evening sky, he had the strangest feeling that they understood.

And so, finally, did he.

The Magic of the Waterfall

If it hadn't been for Emily's insistence, Bea would have found an excuse not to go on the walk, but her granddaughter didn't give her any choice.

"Come on, Granny," she said, jumping up and down while holding on to both her hands. "Come and see the waterfall."

"Yes. Go on, Mum," Kate said. "I'll be fine after a lie-down. It's my own fault for having too many late nights."

"I kept telling you to take it easy," Lewis, Kate's husband, put in. "You were just the same when you were expecting Emily, refusing to slow down."

Kate rolled her eyes. "You should definitely go, Mum, if only to make sure Mr Know-It-All, here, doesn't get them both lost."

As if that would ever happen, Bea thought now, following her son-in-law and granddaughter up the track to the woods. If anyone was likely to get them back safely and punctually, it was him, which was a good thing, obviously. Yet, for some reason, she never felt quite at ease with Lewis.

"These things take time," Bob, who'd gone into town today, had said when she'd mentioned it. "Give the lad a chance."

"They've been married for five years now. How much time does it need? We were always at ease with Ian."

"That's because they grew up together. Lewis has had to start from square one with us, and we've been just as much an unknown quantity to him."

Bea still felt bad about Ian. The youngest son of a local farmer, he and Kate had been close friends all the way through school. When they'd become teenage sweethearts, their path had seemed as clearly marked as this track was now. But while Ian had gone to college locally, unwilling even to contemplate leaving the mountains and fells of his beloved Lake District, Kate had been eager to venture further afield. Bea had encouraged her, as the university place she had been offered was an opportunity not to be missed, but she'd always envisaged her daughter would return afterwards.

Looking back, had she got it wrong?

The path grew narrower and steeper as it climbed up through woodland, peppered with rhododendron bushes planted by landowners in previous generations. Emily's little legs were soon clearly struggling, but she showed no sign of giving in. Lewis didn't intervene, just stayed close enough to be there if needed. After a few moments, the little girl mutely reached her hand up to his. He helped her until the path flattened out, when he let her find her own way again. As was usual with him, all had been carried out with the minimum of fuss or apparent effort.

When he turned round to check whether Bea needed assistance, she knew all she had to do was smile, and shake her head, for him to concentrate his full attention on his daughter again and move on.

In fact, in many ways he was almost too good to be true, seeming to cope as comfortably here as he apparently did in his usual, city, habitat. Even his clothes were what she'd expect the best-dressed walker to wear. His walking boots, for instance, were top of the range, guaranteed to pound the most stubborn peaks into submission, while his trousers were well-fitting and made of a "breathable" fabric. By comparison, her own boots, veterans of many rambles, were the colour of mud, even though they hadn't been originally, and her corduroys were worn practically smooth in places.

Little Emily was kitted out with proper walking boots, too. She was proud of them, judging by the way she insisted on walking to and fro across one of the wooden bridges over the stream that currently entertained pretensions of being a river due to recent downpours. Luckily the bridge was covered with chicken-wire mesh so it didn't get slippery, with sturdy rails up to waist high at the sides.

"I'm stamping!" she shouted. "I'm a giant, and this is my bridge." She furrowed her brow to try and look fierce.

"Oh yeah? In that case, I'm the giant's daddy, so everyone had better watch out." Lewis gave a mock roar which provoked delighted squeals from the would-be giantess.

The steep gradient of the path, combined with the racket of the water rushing down the valley, made conversation impossible for the next few minutes, until the path levelled off again, moving in an arc away from the stream. The uproar temporarily faded into the background, muffled by

70

trees and ferns.

The little giantess declared herself worn out and promptly sat down on a boulder, chin in her hands as she disappeared into a world of her own. Kate had been the same at that age. Even growing up, she'd had that extra dimension, remaining impetuous and funny, as well as considerate and kind. Nowadays, though, she seemed more formal, somehow, almost as if in keeping with her husband.

As they all recovered their breath, Lewis put his hands on his waist and turned right round, taking in the scenery.

"I can't believe I never came here before I knew Kate," he said. "The place really gets to you, doesn't it?" He took his phone out of his jacket pocket. "I'll just text her to keep her up to date on our progress. Hopefully she's taking our advice and having a proper rest."

As abruptly as she'd sat down, Emily stood up.

"Are nearly we at the waterfall yet?"

Lewis looked enquiringly at Bea.

"It's not much further," she said. "But we'll have to be careful, because the path will get slippery. You'll have to hold very tight onto Daddy's hand."

She didn't mention that, when the path got too slippery, it wasn't uncommon to need to turn back without seeing the waterfall in all its glory. Hopefully that shouldn't be the case today but, if it was, Emily might have to be disappointed. She wished she'd had some way of checking before they'd set out, but then it was possible to say that about a lot of things.

Should she have thought more carefully before encouraging Kate to go away, for example? She'd certainly wondered, when Kate had decided her path led elsewhere and broken Ian's heart in the process. Bea had felt unable to look him or his parents in the eye for a long time after that. She never saw them now. The last she'd heard was that he was teaching at a primary school over towards Keswick.

Once they'd crossed the final bridge - complete with obligatory stamping - Emily put her hands over her ears. The noise from the waterfall was almost deafening, even though it couldn't be seen yet, hidden round the corner of a cliff-like rock that formed part of the ravine carved out over thousands of years. The path was indeed slippery, but safe enough provided they took care.

71

Suddenly, there it was, plunging from a height of a good forty feet above them, into a churning pool, before charging its way down the hill to join the river in the valley. It was no coincidence that waterfalls were often given the name "Force" round here, thought Bea.

Light reflecting through the fine spray made an intermittent rainbow, while the rocks, ferns and mosses seemed to glow, so that the place felt like a timeless, enchanted grotto. No matter how often she visited, it still made her gasp. She smiled as she saw Emily's mouth fall open, and could sense, even without looking, that Lewis was just as awestruck.

After a while, he switched Emily's hand over to her grandmother's and took out his phone. Bea knew exactly how he felt, but after failing to do the scene justice through countless photographs over the years, she concentrated instead on absorbing as much of it as possible, as if to imprint it on her memory so that it wouldn't fade.

Eventually they carefully picked their way back to the main path. The roar of water receded as they headed further down. The stream that they had thought so loud on their way up seemed but a poor relation now, while the woods' peaty, mossy scent was soothing to both lungs and soul.

At a section where the path edged the stream, Emily sat down and started taking off her boots.

"What are you doing?" Lewis asked.

"Taking off my shoes and socks so I can paddle."

"That's not a good idea. The water's very cold."

"How cold?"

"*Freezing* cold. So cold, your feet might drop off. A giantess without feet would look very silly."

Emily paused, one foot raised a couple of inches off the ground, considering.

"I could pretend my boots are wellies and paddle in them."

"You could, but then you'd get them, and your socks, soaked." Lewis's tone was just the right side of stern for his daughter to stop arguing. Still, she looked longingly at the stream, as he clearly noticed.

"Look," he pointed out. "There's a nice flat slab of rock jutting out. It's just big enough for us both to kneel on and wiggle our fingers in the water."

"But won't my fingers freeze off?"

Bea couldn't help smiling as the memories came flooding back.

"Your mummy used to like sitting on there and playing with the stream," she said. "She even used to insist on eating her picnic there sometimes."

"And she still has all her fingers," Lewis added. "Or she did when I counted them this morning."

Emily giggled as the two of them knelt down and dipped their hands in the unbelievably clear water. At first she pulled hers straight out again, but once she was used to the cold, she became fascinated by the way her fingers appeared so pale when submerged.

Bea, having declined the offer to join them, laughed as the little girl's fascination turned to squeals when Lewis started splashing her, then daring as she splashed him back, followed by more squeals at his mock-fierce roars.

All the play soon had Emily worn out. "Daddy Giant" ended up carrying the little giantess for the rest of the walk. Her head rested against his shoulder, eyes closing despite her best efforts. Hopefully she would enjoy some magical dreams tonight.

As they approached the grey stone house that was home, Bea was puzzled to see an unfamiliar car outside. Was something wrong with Kate, so that she'd needed to call out a doctor?

Lewis must be thinking along the same lines, because he hurried his pace.

"I'm sure she'd have phoned if there was any problem," he muttered.

Then again, Bea remembered, she hadn't replied to his text message.

Her relief on getting indoors and finding Kate sitting at the kitchen table chatting with a young man and woman over mugs of coffee, was tempered by recognising the former to be none other than Ian.

Thankfully, when Kate smiled, there was no sign of any tension.

"Look who it is. My dear old friend Ian, and his girlfriend, Jenny. They bumped into Dad at the market this morning and he suggested they drop in. It's just as well I did stay behind."

Bea was glad to see there was no tension, either, between the two men as introductions were made. The way Jenny and Ian sat closely together spoke volumes. It looked as if he had found the love of his life, after all.

73

"I hear you've been up to the waterfall," said Ian, as Lewis gently lowered Emily into the big old armchair by the Rayburn. "How was it?"

"A real gem," Lewis replied. "It was one of those occasions that made me wish I was an artist. I took plenty of photographs, but none of them will have really captured the experience. They'll be no more than inadequate snapshots."

Perhaps that had been the problem, all along. The occasions Bea had so far spent with her son-in-law had been inadequate snapshots, as he'd so accurately put it, nothing more. It had taken a trip to a place out of time to get beyond the glossy surface, for both of them. That, combined with the easy atmosphere in the room just now, had achieved more in a few hours than the polite visits and family events over several years.

"Jenny and I were wondering if you'd both like to come for a drink," Ian suggested. "We can catch up on each other's news without crowding out Bea's kitchen."

"Well..." Kate looked at Emily, still asleep.

"I'll happily babysit," said Bea. "You all go out and get acquainted."

With the four of them gone, she made herself some coffee and sat down contentedly. She'd seen a softer and more playful side of Lewis today. Hopefully she'd gradually come to know and understand him even better. Although her daughter had changed, it was only to the extent that everyone did as they moved on with their lives. She was glad to see that Ian had moved on, too. He would never have been happy to leave the mountains, while Kate would have been restless if she'd stayed.

The waterfall had worked its magic. She knew that everything she'd learned today wouldn't fade, but remain as clear as the mountain water that even now ran along the valley.

A Different Person

Ellie clung onto the rock face with rapidly numbing fingers and the cold wind whistling round her, and wondered yet again how she had let herself be persuaded to come on this so-called holiday.

It was all Jo's fault. Her friend had fancied trying an outward-bound course in the Lake District, but not by herself.

"I'll look silly, going on my own," she'd argued. "Just think how much good a few days in the fresh air would do you, and all in beautiful surroundings. You'll feel like a different person by the end of it."

To her surprise, Ellie had ended up agreeing. It was time she got more exercise and saw some new faces. She wasn't the most active person at the best of times, and her job was hardly a calorie-burning occupation, sitting at a computer all day.

She'd even enjoyed going round the no-nonsense hiking shop. Having suddenly shot up several inches at fifteen and even now, at the ripe old age of twenty-three, awkward about her size, shopping tended to be at best a chore, at worst a nightmare. Yet she'd had no problem finding outdoor clothes and walking boots to fit. Who knew? Maybe bigger feet made better walkers.

From the moment they'd arrived at the forbidding, grey stone hostel in yesterday's driving rain, though, Ellie had been convinced she'd made a monumental mistake. That conviction deepened now, as she froze, petrified and unable to move.

"You're perfectly safe. That's what the harness and ropes are for, to make sure you can't fall," Matt, their instructor, tried to reassure her, but to no avail. In the end, he climbed up beside her and patiently talked her down, inch by heart-stopping inch.

"Don't worry," he said, once they were back on the ground. "There will be plenty of other activities to try during the week. I'm sure you'll enjoy those."

As if. She silently vowed never to be on such intimate terms with a rock face again.

The next day saw her installed in a canoe and launching out onto the water. At least there wasn't a cold wind this time. There was no wind at all, and no waves to wobble the canoe or Ellie's precarious self-confidence. Mist blanketed the lake with a dreamlike eeriness which, in a strange way, she liked. After a few minutes, she'd even begun to feel pleased with herself.

"Don't go too far, Ellie. I don't want to have to rescue you," Matt called, just as a group of Cubs and Scouts zipped past as if they'd been doing this all their lives.

Thoroughly deflated, she manoeuvred to face back, seeming to take forever under Matt's watchful gaze.

That was when she first noticed the boat-shed, by a muddy section of shore with several boats and dinghies in various states of repair. Kneeling by one of them, paintbrush in hand, a brown and white dog by his side and a big grin on his face, was a scruffy-looking man. He was probably in his late twenties, she reckoned, though it was difficult to tell under all that mess.

"Keep at it," he shouted, cheerily. "You'll get there in the end."

Even the dog stood up and barked, joining in the fun.

Oh, for the mist to come down and cover her from sight. If anything, it was clearing as the sun gradually won through. There was nothing for it but to grit her teeth and concentrate.

"Nice work," Matt commented when she drew up by his feet. "I couldn't have done that last bit better, myself."

Ellie smiled her thanks and looked round to see if the boat painter had noticed.

There was no sign of him. Typical.

The next day saw her at the summit of a fell whose name she couldn't remember, after a long, arduous trek, surrounded by even more mist. No wonder the sheep here seemed so disgruntled. It was all very well Matt saying the view was stunning on a clear day. Ellie wanted a view today.

Even her boots were no longer the godsend they had seemed at first, though she'd been glad more than once of their support round her ankles. She had been puzzled when the kit list had recommended plasters. Now, as her blisters complained, she wondered if she had brought enough.

"Oh, for a nice long soak in a lovely hot bath," she sighed.

"I ache in places I never knew I had before," said Jo. "And to think that at this moment I could be lying on a beach somewhere, soaking up the sun."

The remark stopped Ellie in her tracks.

"Seriously? But this was all your idea. What possessed you?"

Jo looked thoughtful. "I was looking through my photos when it struck me that most of them were similar. You know, sun, sea and sand, with me and other people my age looking much the same, year after year." She paused as they picked their way down. "So this time I promised myself I'd do something different, more challenging."

"Well, we've certainly been challenged here. Why did you ask me along?"

"As I said before, I didn't want to come by myself. We get on well at work, and you seem the sort of person who'd be prepared to have a go at something like this, and more at home in these sorts of conditions. My other friends are fine for a laugh, but they'd probably turn up in high heels and moan constantly about the state of their nails. Don't get me wrong, I love fashion and so on, but there is a limit. Don't you agree?"

Ellie grimaced. "I wouldn't know. Nothing nice seems to fit me. I'm the wrong shape for everything."

"Really? Maybe you've been looking in the wrong shops. Lots of people make that mistake. You seem fine in what you're wearing at the… Oh my goodness!" Jo halted so abruptly, Ellie nearly walked into the back of her. "Isn't that pretty?"

She looked in the direction her friend was pointing. They'd been so busy talking, they hadn't realised how far down they'd come, or how much the mist had cleared. Previously hidden by the clouds and blocked by the lower fells, the lake was in full view. The surface of the water glittered in the late afternoon sunshine, which also lit up the mountains on the far side in sharp, dramatic detail. It was like another world.

Soon everyone was clicking away with their phones and cameras, and chattering happily, the earlier misery forgotten. Ellie lost count of the number of snaps she took, even though she knew there was no way they could do justice to the mystical quality of the landscape before her. No wonder so many artists and poets had come here for inspiration over the years.

After another hour's walking, their weary but contented group finally turned down the track towards the hostel, passing the boatyard Ellie had spotted the previous day. Mr Scruffy Boatman himself was ambling across, this time holding a spanner. He wore a green, moth-eaten jumper and faded corduroys which sagged at his knees, while his dark, tousled hair looked as if it would challenge even the toughest comb. Yet there was something about him. She couldn't help thinking that if he smiled, she'd see a warmer side to him.

"What do you reckon will be on the menu tonight?" asked Jo, jolting her from her thoughts. "I hope it's something good."

"I don't know," Ellie replied. "Cumberland sausage, by any chance?"

"Oh, please, not again. Aren't there any Chinese takeaways round here?"

"What's wrong with Cumberland sausage? It's good local fare."

They both turned to see the mystery man leaning on the gate.

Ellie groaned inwardly. Now he'd have them down as fussy tourists. Even worse, Jo seemed to have temporarily lost the power of speech, leaving it to her to rescue the situation.

"There's nothing wrong with them at all," she managed to say. "It's just that we've already had them for two nights in a row."

To her dismay, he called out across the track.

"Matt! What have you been doing to these poor ladies? They're complaining about the food."

"Sorry." Matt grinned as he walked over. "Our chef's wife's just had a baby, so the rest of us have been doing the cooking while he takes paternity leave, and our repertoire's rather limited. Don't worry. It's Lancashire Hot Pot tonight, the best you've ever tasted."

"Sounds great." Ellie pasted on what she hoped was her brightest smile to mend any bridges that might be in need of it. "We didn't really mean to complain about the food. It was just a misunderstanding."

Scruffy Boatman was already walking away, head down, arms dangling, with his dog following close at his heels. Had he sensed some implied rebuke in her voice for telling Matt what they had said?

Well, what if he did? Perhaps he often had a joke at the expense of tired walkers hobbling past. It was all very well for him, used to scaling mountains and squelching through bogs. She'd like to see him try coping in another environment. Wriggling uncomfortably in a suit, perhaps. She spent a happy moment visualising herself in her smartest clothes, explaining the computer system with exaggerated patience.

Yet her office garb often made her feel restricted and frumpy. Truth to tell, she felt much more at home in the comfortable trousers, fleece tops and strong, waterproof jacket she'd been wearing this week. If only she could wear them all the time.

Almost before she knew it, it was their last day. The group enjoyed an exhilarating morning's sailing, followed by a walk in woodland, where tiny wildflowers peeped out like stars from the moss.

All too soon, it was over and they were once again passing the boatyard. This time there was no sign of its owner. Ellie scanned the lake. Perhaps he'd taken one of the boats out on the water?

"Looking for Doug?"

She hadn't realised Matt was so close by.

"He's at the accountants' today," he continued. "Probably won't be back till later this evening.'

"Is the boat-building business his own, then?" Ellie couldn't help asking.

"That's right. He's always enjoyed tinkering with boats, even at school. Well, more than tinkering. He's really skilled. A couple of years ago he took the plunge, and now he's pretty much inundated. Between you and me, he works too hard."

Even though she couldn't explain why, she felt sad to have missed him.

As they reached the hostel, Ellie and Jo both paused for a last look across the lake to the distant fells.

"I've enjoyed this week," Jo commented. "I'll be glad to get home, though."

A couple of days earlier, Ellie would have said the same.

At least there was still the night out for everyone to look forward to, at the pub in the village.

With its slate floors and stone walls, the place was warm and welcoming. Potted geraniums adorned deep windowsills, a game of skittles was under way in one corner, and several dogs lay comfortably on the floor – a certain brown and white one among them. On seeing the group, its owner waved and came over.

He was dressed as ever in corduroys and a jumper, this time with no sags or holes, or even a smudge of oil in sight. His hair, although still a little on the unruly side, had been relentlessly combed into near submission. He was also, Ellie noticed, a good couple of inches taller than her, now that he wasn't slouching or leaning on anything.

To her surprise, he held out his hand.

"We've already met a couple of times, but I didn't get round to introducing myself," he said. "As you may have noticed, I'm not very adept at that sort of thing."

His handshake was warm and firm. Matt had gone to fetch a round of drinks, while Jo had been dragged off to make up the numbers of a game of darts in the next room, leaving the two of them alone.

"Anyway, I'm Doug," he added. "And this is Milly, my constant companion."

The dog thumped her tail at the mention of her name.

Doug hesitated and shifted awkwardly.

"I believe I owe you an apology for my behaviour the other day. Me and Matt were just larking about. It didn't mean anything, but I can understand how it can take a bit of getting used to. I didn't realise till afterwards that you might not have seen it that way." He smiled slowly. Ellie had been right about his smile. "By the way, will you ever be able to face Cumberland sausage again?"

"Absolutely. The only trouble is, the taste will make me want to take the next train back here. Even with only being here for a short while, I've fallen in love with the place. I don't know what it is, but I just feel... right here, somehow."

Doug nodded as Matt came back with their drinks. "I know what you mean. I could never imagine living anywhere else."

"Same here," Matt agreed, once they'd filled him in on the conversation. "The pull of this place is so strong, it's almost physical."

That was it in a nutshell, Ellie realised as she took a long draught from her pint of local bitter. Matt had put into words the feeling that had been quietly growing in her over the last couple of days. She hated the thought that the Lakes might become a distant memory.

"How did you get on with the accountant?" Matt asked, changing the subject.

Doug shrugged his shoulders. "Pretty much as expected. The business is expanding, which is good news, but I've got to keep on top of the paperwork. I'm never going to manage that. There aren't enough hours in the day, even apart from the fact that I'm lousy at that side of things."

Ellie stroked Milly's silky head as the conversation unfolded and an idea took seed in her mind. Doug might not be very good at the administration involved in running a business, but she could practically do it with her eyes closed. Only last month, she'd been promoted and told that if she stayed where she was working now, her prospects were excellent. Her future was safely mapped out in gentle slopes and well-marked routes, so unlike the squashed brown contour lines and dotted paths of the maps around here. She'd be mad to give that up for the sake of a dream. Wouldn't she?

Then again...

She turned to Doug.

"Can I ask you something?"

Matt checked Ellie's harness before sorting out his own.

"Are you sure you need to do this?" he asked. "Doug's already said the job's yours if you want it. He practically fell off his chair when you told him your qualifications and experience."

"It's difficult to explain," Ellie replied, "but I've sort of struck a bargain with myself. If I can master this, it's a sign that I should stay. If not, then maybe it's not the life for me. I know that might not sound logical, but there you go. Anyway, I've already cancelled my rail ticket and stumped up extra for a later one, so we might as well get on with it."

Still, for all her bravado, she could feel her doubts, not to mention outright fear, mount at the same rate as her hands grew clammy.

Trembling, she eased herself up the rock face, focusing on Matt's instructions and trying not to think of the long climb and all that empty, stomach-churning space below once she got anywhere.

"Remember to always maintain three points of contact, and you'll be okay," said Matt.

Three? Eight might just about be enough. For the first time in her life, she envied spiders.

With a deep, shuddering breath, Ellie forced her right arm to move, watching her fingers scrabble for a hold. Found one. She stretched her right leg, feeling with the front of her boot for a toehold that would support her to the next stage.

Thank goodness. That was her right foot sorted out. Left hand next, then left foot. Slowly, slowly. She'd managed everything else this week. She could manage this. She had to. It had suddenly become the most important thing in the world.

It seemed an age before she reached the top of the rock face. Absolutely exhausted, she pulled herself over the top and could have kissed the ground, but instead sank down on her hands and knees.

Matt, of course, climbed up effortlessly.

"Well done," he said, kneeling down beside her and putting one arm round her shoulders. "It looked a bit iffy at a couple of points there, but you persisted. You must really want to live here."

Ellie got shakily to her feet, leaning on a lovely big boulder for support.

"Thank you. I could never have done it without your help."

Her throat swelled with emotion as she gazed at the view. Settlements nestled, cocooned by the mountains from the world outside. She could recognise some of them even now. There was the Old Man of Coniston, with his conical summit, and the dramatic outline of Dow Crag just beyond. Already they felt like old friends.

"What's the reception like up here?" she asked when she was able to speak.

Matt checked his phone. "Okay, actually. Would you like me to do the honours?" Before she could change her mind, he was already dialling.

"Hey, Doug. Guess what? I'm half way up a mountain with someone who'd like to speak to you."

"He's all yours," he winked as he handed the phone to her.

Ellie took a deep breath.

"It's me," she said. "If that offer's still open, I'd like to take it."

Rescue Me

"Oh, no. No, no, no. Not here, of all places!"

I could protest to empty space as much as I liked. It made no difference.

I'd grown up in the Lake District. I'd had rules about staying safe on the fells drummed into me, practically from the cradle. I even had a responsible job. Yet here I was, on one of the passes, surrounded by wilderness, in a broken-down car.

Clouds were already congregating over the crags as I shivered in my office clothes. When I'd set out, it had been a beautiful day, full of the promise of spring round the corner. But everyone, even non-locals, knew that Lakeland weather could change in an instant.

At least I wasn't the only person to have been lulled into a false sense of security. Clive, the senior partner in the firm of solicitors where I worked, had let himself be deceived, too. Then again, his view was probably influenced by possessing a well-built Range Rover, while I drove an old run-around that had just chosen one of the worst moments to decide it didn't fancy running around any more, thank you very much.

"I don't suppose you could go out and see old Bill Bryant for me, could you, Mandy?" he'd asked.

Bill, a sheep farmer, whose sons ran the farm now that he couldn't get about so well, was one of the firm's oldest clients. This earned him extra attention, including having his new will taken to him to be signed and witnessed. The fact that it gave Clive a rare excuse for a drive out and a good old natter may also have had something to do with it.

That had been the plan, anyway, until Clive had phoned the office, earlier that morning.

"I'm stuck at court, I'm afraid. The case before ours is dragging on a bit. I'd rearrange the appointment, but Bill's sorted out two people to witness him signing, so we'd end up messing them about, too. It's a nice day for an outing," he'd added, persuasively.

When your boss asks for a favour, you generally oblige, don't you? And it had indeed been an enjoyable drive. I'd been made most welcome at the farm, where Bill had turned out to be a great teller of tales over tea and home made fruit cake.

Then, heading back over the fells, there'd been an ominous clunk, followed by the sound of rubber battling tarmac as one of the back wheels locked up, barely giving me time to pull in to what almost counted as a passing spot at the side of the single track road.

The silence on the fells can be eerie, and that's how it was now, interrupted only by the wind moaning round the slopes, and the tremulous bleats of sheep drifting up from the valley where they were sheltered from the worst of winter. And not a soul in sight.

Thank goodness for mobile phones. I pulled mine from my handbag, ready to call out the breakdown service, only to find it was dead. I'd meant to charge it up overnight but had completely forgotten. There was nothing for it but to pick up my bag, pull my inadequate coat round me and start walking in search of the nearest farm.

"It could have been worse," I told myself. "It could have been in the middle of winter, not near the end. Or later in the day, when it gets dark."

I must have gone about fifty yards when I became aware of a new, discordant sound, and looked back to see an elderly Land Rover appear over the nearest rise. The vehicle's snarl changed down to the throb of an idling engine as it pulled up beside me and the driver wound down his window.

"Is everything all right?"

"Just problems with the car." I tried to sound confident and authoritative, aware that I was alone on a fell road. "I'm on my way to a nearby farm to call out the breakdown service."

"You'll have a fair old walk, then. I can probably help. Me and my brother run a garage. Don't worry, it's all above board." He passed a business card to me out of the window. "Is that your car, back there? Let's have a look. I'll reverse back and you can catch me up."

"Sounds like the wheel bearing's gone," Jake, as he'd introduced himself, said a few minutes later, when I'd described what had happened.

His dark hair, open face and stocky build suited both him and his surroundings. He seemed completely at home out here, and there weren't many people I could have said that about. I reckoned he was probably in his late twenties, like me. Unlike me, he was clearly practical.

84

"I can't do anything here, but we can fix it at our garage for a reasonable price. I'll call my brother to come out with the truck."

"Oh, there's no need," I said. "If I could borrow your phone, I can call out the breakdown service. You've been a great help."

He shook his head. "The signal's rubbish up here. They'll only ask us to fetch the car, anyway. Our best bet is to drive to the pub at the bottom and use their phone."

The pub was typical of many in the area, with thick, solid walls and a stone-flagged floor. The sight of huge plates of Cumberland sausage and chips being served at several tables reminded me it was lunchtime, so we agreed we may as well have a bite to eat, though we settled for sandwiches. Even those were substantial, suited to walkers' appetites, as well as tasty.

"Our dad set up the garage about thirty years ago," Jake told me as we both tucked in. "We're always busy with repairs. We sell second hand Land Rovers and Range Rovers, too. They're vital for getting around in bad weather, and not everyone wants to splash out on a brand new model. Clive's a customer of ours, and vice versa. Your receptionist's even a cousin of our mum's. I don't recall seeing you before, though."

"That's because I've only been there for a couple of months," I said. "I went away at eighteen to go to university, and I've worked in Manchester ever since."

"And yet you're here." He raised his eyebrows.

"I… grew tired of city life. I saw this job advertised and applied for it, practically on the spur of the moment. When I travelled up for the interview, the mountains already had snow on the tops. It almost felt as if they'd been waiting for me." I felt my cheeks redden. "Sorry. That must sound weird."

"No, it doesn't," said Jake. "I feel the same whenever I've been away. So I take it you didn't hesitate when they offered you the post?"

I nodded, relieved that he understood. "The only drawback is that I'm living with my parents again. We get on well, but after being away for several years, it feels very strange. I can't afford a place of my own, and any house shares I've come across either clearly wouldn't work out or are too far away."

"House shares can be tricky," Jake agreed. "I'm lucky. I share with my brother, Sam. Our sister shares a house, too. I think they might have a

85

room coming free. I can ask her for you, if that's any help." He glanced up. "Talk of the devil. Looks like Sam's arrived."

A taller, lankier version of Jake approached our table and helped himself to some of Jake's side portion of chips after we'd been introduced.

"I had to deal with a call-out on the Barrow road, so I only had time for a quick cheese and pickle sandwich for lunch," he explained, as he added more vinegar.

"Yeah, and I bet you're wasting away." Jake rolled his eyes. "Anyway, if you can pick up Mandy's car, I'll drive her back to work, then head on to the garage and get on with some of the jobs there."

The journey passed quickly, probably because Jake knew the roads well and the Land Rover's height gave a better view ahead. Warm, weathered grey houses and farms looked as if they'd grown out of the earth, while dry-stone walls zigzagged up impossibly steep slopes where sheep grazed unconcernedly.

Back in the town, I felt a sudden, inexplicable pang as I watched him drive away after he'd dropped me off, but I gave myself a shake. I'd be avoiding any entanglements for a long, long time. Despite what I'd told him, tiredness of city life wasn't the only reason I'd come back.

"Ah, they're good lads," Angela, our receptionist, said when I told her about my little adventure. "I supposed I'm biased, being related. Still, your car's in safe hands with Jake. He won't charge you an arm and a leg, either."

I didn't need to get out and about for any appointments over the rest of the week, and even got a lift to and from work. For all that, I was glad when I came down to reception and Angela presented me with my car key and an envelope containing an invoice. Even that wasn't too painful, coming comfortably within the amount my dad had warned me was likely.

"Your car's in the car park, just in time for the weekend," she told me. "Jake brought it round himself. He wanted to go through the details with you, but you were with a client. Oh, and he left his business card with his number, in case you need him again. I always take my car to him."

"He should pay you commission," I joked. "I must say, he's keen. This is the second card of his I've got."

"It's funny how these things work out, isn't it?" Angela said as I turned to go back to my office. "If your car hadn't broken down when it did, and Jake hadn't been passing, you wouldn't have met. And all because Clive got held up at court."

"Life's full of coincidences," I replied, wondering why she was looking at me so closely. Had my disappointment at missing him shown on my face? "I know one thing that won't be a coincidence, though. If I don't get on with some work, there are going to be some unhappy clients."

Anyway, I reflected, as I caught up with some emails, why shouldn't I be a bit disappointed? However wonderful it was to be back in a place I loved, my social life wasn't exactly sizzling.

My thoughts were interrupted by a name on one of the emails. It was Martin's work email address rather than his private one, but that didn't stop my heart from pounding as I opened the message.

Hi Mandy, it read. *How's the new job? It's as crazy as ever here. I've got a case at one of your local courts next Friday. I never knew they had such things in the back of beyond, but it means I'll be in the area. One of my friends has a yacht on Windermere and a weekend cottage nearby, so I should be able to stay over with him. Fancy meeting up for old times' sake?*

It was lucky the rest of the work I had that afternoon was fairly routine, because I'm not sure I could have concentrated on anything more taxing. On the other hand, that might have helped to stop my thoughts continually flicking back to what he'd written.

Martin was the main cause of my coming home to lick my wounds. After nearly a year together, he'd decided "it wasn't working", and broken my heart. Yet now, not only was he contacting me, but specifically hinting he'd be up for the weekend.

I was still distracted at the end of the day. So much so, that I'd driven most of the way home before I realised I didn't recognise the music coming from my CD player. Or, rather, I did, because I'd heard it before and liked it, but it wasn't in my collection. I let it continue playing, only taking out the disc once I'd pulled up onto my parents' drive, before dialling the number on one of the two identical business cards in my bag.

"What an idiot I am. I put it in your player when I drove the car to your office, and then forgot all about it," Jake said when I handed the disc over to him, that evening. "This lot haven't stopped teasing me. Remind me never to listen to my voicemails in their presence again."

"This lot" turned out to be Sam, their sister, Tracey, and her boyfriend, Joe. Jake had suggested I join them where they were all meeting up for a Friday night drink.

"Nothing fancy," he'd said. "Just a way to unwind after a busy week."

Despite being tired, I was glad I'd agreed to go along. They were a friendly bunch. I soon felt brighter than I had for a good while.

"I hear you're looking for somewhere with a room to rent," said Tracey. "One of my housemates is getting married soon, so she'll be moving out. Unless the wedding's called off at the last minute, or something." Was it my imagination, or did she glance at Jake as she said that? "It's a nice house, the rent's reasonable, and it's not too far from here. I can mention it to our landlord, if you're interested."

"That would be brilliant," I said. "Thanks."

We all got on so well, the evening flew by.

"We must do this again some time," said Jake, as we all left. But it was me he said it to, as he walked me back to my car.

"Yes, we must," I found myself agreeing. "It was fun."

The second email from Martin appeared on Monday afternoon.

Hi Mandy. Didn't you get my last email? I suppose that's what comes of being out in the sticks. My mate at Windermere's been in touch. It's fine for me to stay next weekend. We might even get out on the yacht. You're invited, too, by the way. Say you'll meet me on Friday. I'll treat you to a meal so we can have a proper talk. It's not been the same without you. Martin x

I could hardly believe what I was reading. Was this the same Martin who'd said we were too different? Maybe I was wrong, and he just wanted to get together as old friends, but so much in his message suggested otherwise. If he'd sent something like this to me two months ago, I'd have jumped at the invitation. Even now, despite all my resolutions, I could feel the past tugging at me.

I took a deep breath.

I'll think about it, I typed, with trembling fingers.

I was my own person now, I told myself. Even if I did meet him, it would be on my terms.

And I'd pay for my own meal.

Pay? I froze as I realised I'd forgotten to pay Jake for the repairs. What must he think? Within seconds, I was rummaging in my bag.

"We must stop meeting like this," Jake teased when we met up for a coffee at a nearby hotel bar, after work. "It's getting to be a habit."

"I'm so sorry," I replied, as I wrote out a cheque. "I meant to pay you on Friday night, but I clean forgot."

"So did I. We all enjoyed ourselves, that's the main thing." He looked more closely at me. "Are you okay? You look a bit flustered. Bad day at the office?"

I sighed. "Sort of."

"Ooh, that sounded heart-felt."

"It's complicated."

"Oh dear." He paused. "Tell you what, if it helps take your mind off things, do you fancy coming for a pizza, one night? One of Sam's friends is having a party at his dad's farm next Saturday, as well. You're welcome to come to that. It's a bit out in the wilds, but we'll be fine in the Land Rover."

I slumped back in my chair.

"Oh, Jake. That sounds wonderful, but it makes things even more complicated."

"Something really is bothering you, isn't it? I can be a sympathetic listener, you know. If you want to tell me, that is. Shall I get us a couple more coffees?"

And so, after he'd come back with our drinks and a generous slab of chocolate cake, I did.

Jake didn't interrupt or joke even once, but waited in silence till I'd finished.

"It sounds like you've had a tough time. If it's any help, I think you were right to make a fresh start. The question is, do you want to slide backwards again?"

"Of course I don't. Only…" My throat felt too full to speak.

"Would it help to hear of my experience?"

I looked up as Jake took several gulps of his coffee, as if preparing himself.

"The thing is, I've been in a similar situation," he began. "We were even engaged, but she changed her mind. It was a blow. To tell the truth, without the support of my friends and family, I'm not sure how I'd

89

have coped." I remembered the way his sister had glanced at him, that other evening. "Then she changed her mind. Again. Said she'd made a mistake. My friends warned me to steer clear, but I suppose a part of me was flattered. So I undid all that hard work and started seeing her again. I think you can guess what happened next. It just re-opened old wounds."

Impulsively, I put my hand over his.

"You remember you said it felt as if the mountains had been waiting for you to come back?" Jake continued, after a moment. "Well, for a while I felt as if they were my best friends. They didn't judge. They didn't tell me things would get better. They were just there. Does that sound mad?"

I smiled. "You know it doesn't."

As I said the words, I thought of Martin and how the notion would have sounded completely crazy to him. Maybe he'd been right. We were too different.

"I got over it, eventually, but the whole experience made me extra wary of getting involved with anyone again." Our eyes met. "Until I met you."

For the next few moments it felt as if we were the only people there. I was aware of the babble of background chatter, and the crackling of logs on the fire, but they all seemed far away, as if part of a dream. Only Jake's voice came through clearly.

"Obviously, it's none of my business what you decide to do about this Martin bloke. Whatever you do, I hope it works out. All I will say is that it seems to me he doesn't deserve you." He swallowed. "It's taken me a long time to start trusting my feelings again, but the thing is, I really enjoy your company and I'd love to spend more time with you. And if you'd rather it was just as friends for now, that's fine by me." His mouth curved into a half smile. "Maybe there's something about us. People can't stay away from either of us, even after they've left."

'Or we can't stay away from each other,' I thought.

It was true, almost as if the fells themselves had conspired to bring us together.

Out loud, I said, "That would suit me very well, because I enjoy your company, too. I'd love to come to that party. And how did you know pizza's my favourite food?"

His eyes crinkled.

"Isn't it everybody's?"

I stood up.

"Do you know what? All this talk of food is making me hungry. Is there a decent chip shop nearby?"

His eyes crinkled even more. "There's one just down the road, the best for miles. We can get some chips and meet up with the others. We'll need plenty, though. You'd be amazed how much my sister can put away."

"So your ex-boyfriend's friend has a yacht, does he?" he continued, once we were outside. "I've got a canoe I sometimes take on Coniston Water, but I don't suppose that compares. If you don't want to meet up with him, I could take up the offer. I've always fancied a taste of the high life."

As I laughed at the thought of how Jake would react to Martin – and vice versa, as Jake would say - I knew how I'd reply to Martin's email. In the meantime, Jake's hand holding mine as we walked was warm and reassuring, adding to the sense of having truly come home, and the knowledge that I was ready to start trusting my feelings again, too, just as Jake had, even if only a little at a time.

And if the road ahead was rough? Well, we always had Jake's Land Rover to cope with any difficult terrain.

Dreaming Is Free

The old farmhouse looked empty and yet at home in the Lakeland landscape, its grey stone nestling comfortably into the sheep-cropped green of the fells rising behind it.

Someone, perhaps a farmer's wife, had once tended a garden, judging by a small rectangle of richer grass separated from the tougher version by a low, dry-stone wall. A sign marked "Private Land" discouraged anyone from going closer, but even from this distance Diane could see several spots of delicate pink swaying in the breeze. Roses. Whoever had lived here had loved flowers, too.

"Are you dreaming again?" Tom's laugh broke into her thoughts.

"Well, aren't you?" she replied. "Remember all the times we said we'd live up here, and visualised our perfect house?"

"And remember all the times we agreed we couldn't live on fresh air?"

It was her turn to laugh. "That's true. But dreaming is free."

The fact that they'd come walking this way by chance only seemed to add to the magic. They'd spent the first half of the day enjoying a picnic by the lake and making the most of the unseasonably warm weather, which would probably be the last of the year.

By early afternoon, that had changed. As if autumn had suddenly remembered it was due, the breeze had picked up, bringing a sudden chill to the air. It seemed only a matter of minutes from their listening to the water lapping at the shore, to its being whipped into little white horses.

"I'd like to see you trying to skim stones across the surface now," Diane joked, raising her voice to be heard over the rustle of the leaves, as they packed away their picnic and books and put on warmer tops.

"Let's not leave yet," said Tom. "We might not be back again for a while. There's a path through the woods that we've never really explored. According to the map, it heads up onto the fell, where there should be some good views. The weather may have turned cooler, but it's still fine."

They put everything back in the car and got out their walking

93

boots, as well as a rucksack containing waterproofs and extra layers of clothing, just in case, before they set off on the path through the deciduous woods cloaking the sheltered lower slopes.

Almost thirty years had passed since they'd met at a wedding in Kendal, falling in love both with each other and the Lake District at the same time. Since then, they'd come back again and again, including a stay for their honeymoon.

When the children arrived, it was only natural that they should be introduced to the place, too. Diane could still remember, as if it were yesterday, each of them lying on a rug by her on the stony shore, waving their chubby, bare arms and legs in the soft air on warmer days as the mountains looked on benignly.

Now the owners of those no-longer-so-chubby limbs were adults, forging their own dreams.

Dreams. Diane smiled to herself. Tom might sometimes laugh, but there was nothing wrong with a little dreaming, was there? Not that they made her any less attentive to day-to-day matters. They just gave everything that little extra sweetness. Wasn't that why so many people came for holidays here, to live out a little of their dreams and go home replenished with a fresh supply?

After a stiff climb, they emerged onto an upper track and into bright sunlight.

"How's that for a view?" Tom panted.

Diane leaned on a former gatepost as she took it all in. Ahead of them, the fell stretched ever upwards. Below, beyond the belt of trees in their glowing autumn colours, two white yachts the size of moths hardly seemed to move on the inky-blue lake.

It was when she turned round that she noticed the farmhouse, about four hundred yards away at the end of the track the missing gate would once have closed off. The grass, the roses, the little garden wall - they were all there. She could almost imagine sheets flapping on a washing line, and a woman carrying a bag of wooden clothes pegs while two children clung to her skirt and a cat curled up in a sunny spot on one of the window sills.

Tom's thoughtful expression indicated the place was casting a spell on him, too.

"This track must join on to the road further along the valley," he said, after a moment. "It probably comes out at the section just before the woods start."

"As if we'd ever get the car up here," Diane retorted.

"We wouldn't. I'd change it for a four by four."

"Now who's dreaming? And it's a long way to the shops."

"What do you think freezers were invented for? Besides, we'd never be short of fresh mutton."

"Tom!" Diane slapped his arm playfully. "Look, even that sheep's glaring at you, and I don't blame it. Don't listen to him," she told the astonished-looking animal, which responded by turning tail and trotting off.

"Don't worry. Sheep-rustling isn't one of my ambitions. I wouldn't want to end up faced with an irate farmer."

By now the scene was already changing, the mountains reddening in the late afternoon light. The days were shortening quickly now.

"Irate farmer or not," Diane pointed out. "If we don't start back soon, it'll be dark by the time we get to the car."

It felt good to be home, Diane thought, a couple of weeks later. Sheets really did flap on the line in their garden. It helped that the weather was still just about up to hanging out the washing.

"It would be cold and probably misty on the fells by now," Tom had reminded her, just that morning, as their kitchen filled with the aroma of freshly filtered coffee. "And raining. Let's face it, how do you think the lakes have so much water?"

There had been mist over the fields here, too, first thing, making everything diaphanous and mysterious, and the countryside all the more precious when it cleared.

"Our local scenery may not be spectacular, but I still like it," Tom had commented as they'd driven to a nearby market town, the previous Saturday.

Gazing across at the bronze trees and golden fields rolling out from each side of the road, Diane couldn't help but agree.

Even as she went through the photos of their recent holiday, she realised that, in all the most important ways, her dreams were already fulfilled. She had people she loved around her, as well as a comfortable home and pretty garden.

All of that didn't stop her having other dreams, of course.

Speaking of which, that reminded her there was something she

95

needed to do.

Diane checked her watch. If she set off now, she should get to the garden centre in good time before it closed. This was the best time of year to purchase and plant roses.

Including delicate pink ones, as similar as possible to the colour she'd seen by a certain Lakeland farmhouse, with the fells rising above it on one side, the woods and lake below on the other, and signs of a once-lovingly tended garden.